Big Blonde

Dorothy Parker

Big Blonde

PENGUIN CLASSICS
an imprint of
PENGUIN BOOKS

PENGUIN CLASSICS

UK | USA | Canada | Ireland | Australia
India | New Zealand | South Africa

Penguin Books is part of the Penguin Random House group of companies
whose addresses can be found at global.penguinrandomhouse.com.

Penguin
Random House
UK

These stories first appeared in *The New Yorker, Smart Set, Harper's Bazaar,
Mercury, Pictorial Review* and *The Bookman* between 1922 and 1941. Selections for
this edition taken from *Complete Stories*, Penguin Classics, 2003.
This selection published in Little Clothbound Classics 2022

001

Cover design and illustration by Coralie Bickford-Smith

Set in 9.5/13pt Baskerville 10 Pro
Typeset by Jouve (UK), Milton Keynes
Printed and bound in Great Britain by Clays Ltd, Elcograf S.p.A.

The authorized representative in the EEA is Penguin Random House Ireland,
Morrison Chambers, 32 Nassau Street, Dublin DO2 YH68

A CIP catalogue record for this book is available from the British Library

ISBN: 978-0-241-60993-4

www.greenpenguin.co.uk

Contents

The Standard of Living

Annabel and Midge came out of the tea room with the arrogant slow gait of the leisured, for their Saturday afternoon stretched ahead of them. They had lunched, as was their wont, on sugar, starches, oils, and butter-fats. Usually they ate sandwiches of spongy new white bread greased with butter and mayonnaise; they ate thick wedges of cake lying wet beneath ice cream and whipped cream and melted chocolate gritty with nuts. As alternates, they ate patties, sweating beads of inferior oil, containing bits of bland meat bogged in pale, stiffening sauce; they ate pastries, limber under rigid icing, filled with an indeterminate yellow sweet stuff, not still solid, not yet liquid, like salve that has been left in the sun. They chose no other sort of food, nor did they consider it. And their skin was like the petals of wood anemones, and their bellies were as flat and their flanks as lean as those of young Indian braves.

Annabel and Midge had been best friends almost from the day that Midge had found a job as stenographer with the firm that employed Annabel. By now, Annabel, two years longer in the stenographic department, had worked up to the wages of eighteen dollars and fifty cents a week; Midge was still at sixteen dollars. Each girl lived at home with her family and paid half her salary to its support.

The girls sat side by side at their desks, they lunched together every noon, together they set out for home at the end of the day's work. Many of their evenings and most of their Sundays were passed in each other's company. Often they were joined by two young men, but there was no steadiness to any such quartet; the two young men would give place, unlamented, to two other young men, and lament would have been inappropriate, really, since the newcomers were scarcely distinguishable from their predecessors. Invariably the girls spent the fine idle hours of their hot-weather Saturday afternoons together. Constant use had not worn ragged the fabric of their friendship.

They looked alike, though the resemblance did not lie in their features. It was in the shape of their bodies, their movements, their style, and their adornments. Annabel and Midge did, and completely, all that young office workers are besought not to do. They painted their lips and their nails, they darkened their lashes and lightened their hair, and scent seemed to shimmer from them. They wore thin, bright dresses, tight over their breasts and high on their legs, and tilted slippers, fancifully strapped. They looked conspicuous and cheap and charming.

Now, as they walked across to Fifth Avenue with their skirts swirled by the hot wind, they received audible admiration. Young men grouped lethargically about

newsstands awarded them murmurs, exclamations, even –
the ultimate tribute – whistles. Annabel and Midge passed
without the condescension of hurrying their pace; they
held their heads higher and set their feet with exquisite
precision, as if they stepped over the necks of peasants.

Always the girls went to walk on Fifth Avenue on their
free afternoons, for it was the ideal ground for their
favorite game. The game could be played anywhere, and,
indeed, was, but the great shop windows stimulated the
two players to their best form.

Annabel had invented the game; or rather she had
evolved it from an old one. Basically, it was no more than
the ancient sport of what-would-you-do-if-you-had-a-
million-dollars? But Annabel had drawn a new set of rules
for it, had narrowed it, pointed it, made it stricter. Like
all games, it was the more absorbing for being more
difficult.

Annabel's version went like this: You must suppose
that somebody dies and leaves you a million dollars, cool.
But there is a condition to the bequest. It is stated in the
will that you must spend every nickel of the money on
yourself.

There lay the hazard of the game. If, when playing it,
you forgot, and listed among your expenditures the rental
of a new apartment for your family, for example, you lost
your turn to the other player. It was astonishing how
many – and some of them among the experts, too – would
forfeit all their innings by such slips.

It was essential, of course, that it be played in passionate seriousness. Each purchase must be carefully considered and, if necessary, supported by argument. There was no zest to playing wildly. Once Annabel had introduced the game to Sylvia, another girl who worked in the office. She explained the rules to Sylvia and then offered her the gambit 'What would be the first thing you'd do?' Sylvia had not shown the decency of even a second of hesitation. 'Well,' she said, 'the first thing I'd do, I'd go out and hire somebody to shoot Mrs Gary Cooper, and then . . .' So it is to be seen that she was no fun.

But Annable and Midge were surely born to be comrades, for Midge played the game like a master from the moment she learned it. It was she who added the touches that made the whole thing cozier. According to Midge's innovations, the eccentric who died and left you the money was not anybody you loved, or, for the matter of that, anybody you even knew. It was somebody who had seen you somewhere and had thought, 'That girl ought to have lots of nice things. I'm going to leave her a million dollars when I die.' And the death was to be neither untimely nor painful. Your benefactor, full of years and comfortably ready to depart, was to slip softly away during sleep and go right to heaven. These embroideries permitted Annabel and Midge to play their game in the luxury of peaceful consciences.

Midge played with a seriousness that was not only proper but extreme. The single strain on the girls' friendship had followed an announcement once made by Annabel that the first thing she would buy with her million dollars would be a silver-fox coat. It was as if she had struck Midge across the mouth. When Midge recovered her breath, she cried that she couldn't imagine how Annabel could do such a thing – silver-fox coats were common! Annabel defended her taste with the retort that they were not common, either. Midge then said that they were so. She added that everybody had a silver-fox coat. She went on, with perhaps a slight loss of head, to declare that she herself wouldn't be caught dead in silver fox.

For the next few days, though the girls saw each other as constantly, their conversation was careful and infrequent, and they did not once play their game. Then one morning, as soon as Annabel entered the office, she came to Midge and said that she had changed her mind. She would not buy a silver-fox coat with any part of her million dollars. Immediately on receiving the legacy, she would select a coat of mink.

Midge smiled and her eyes shone. 'I think,' she said, 'you're doing absolutely the right thing.'

Now, as they walked along Fifth Avenue, they played the game anew. It was one of those days with which September is repeatedly cursed; hot and glaring, with slivers of dust in the wind. People drooped and shambled, but the girls carried themselves tall and walked a straight line, as befitted young heiresses on their afternoon promenade. There was no longer need for them to start the

5

game at its formal opening. Annabel went direct to the heart of it.

'All right,' she said. 'So you've got this million dollars. So what would be the first thing you'd do?'

'Well, the first thing I'd do,' Midge said, 'I'd get a mink coat.' But she said it mechanically, as if she were giving the memorized answer to an expected question.

'Yes,' Annabel said, 'I think you ought to. The terribly dark kind of mink.' But she, too, spoke as if by rote. It was too hot; fur, no matter how dark and sleek and supple, was horrid to the thoughts.

They stepped along in silence for a while. Then Midge's eye was caught by a shop window. Cool, lovely gleamings were there set off by chaste and elegant darkness.

'No,' Midge said, 'I take it back. I wouldn't get a mink coat the first thing. Know what I'd do? I'd get a string of pearls. Real pearls.'

Annabel's eyes turned to follow Midge's.

'Yes,' she said, slowly. 'I think that's kind of a good idea. And it would make sense, too. Because you can wear pearls with anything.'

Together they went over to the shop window and stood pressed against it. It contained but one object – a double row of great, even pearls clasped by a deep emerald around a little pink velvet throat.

'What do you suppose they cost?' Annabel said.

'Gee, I don't know,' Midge said. 'Plenty, I guess.'

'Like a thousand dollars?' Annabel said.

'Oh, I guess like more,' Midge said. 'On account of the emerald.'

'Well, like ten thousand dollars?' Annabel said.

'Gee, I wouldn't even know,' Midge said.

The devil nudged Annabel in the ribs. 'Dare you to go in and price them,' she said.

'Like fun!' Midge said.

'Dare you,' Annabel said.

'Why, a store like this wouldn't even be open this afternoon,' Midge said.

'Yes, it is so, too,' Annabel said. 'People just came out. And there's a doorman on. Dare you.'

'Well,' Midge said. 'But you've got to come too.'

They tendered thanks, icily, to the doorman for ushering them into the shop. It was cool and quiet, a broad, gracious room with paneled walls and soft carpet. But the girls wore expressions of bitter disdain, as if they stood in a sty.

A slim, immaculate clerk came to them and bowed. His neat face showed no astonishment at their appearance.

'Good afternoon,' he said. He implied that he would never forget it if they would grant him the favor of accepting his soft-spoken greeting.

'Good afternoon,' Annabel and Midge said together, and in like freezing accents.

'Is there something – ?' the clerk said.

'Oh, we're just looking,' Annabel said. It was as if she flung the words down from a dais.

7

The clerk bowed.

'My friend and myself merely happened to be passing,' Midge said, and stopped, seeming to listen to the phrase. 'My friend here and myself,' she went on, 'merely happened to be wondering how much are those pearls you've got in your window.'

'Ah, yes,' the clerk said. 'The double rope. That is two hundred and fifty thousand dollars, Madam.'

'I see,' Midge said.

The clerk bowed. 'An exceptionally beautiful necklace,' he said 'Would you care to look at it?'

'No, thank you,' Annabel said.

'My friend and myself merely happened to be passing,' Midge said.

They turned to go; to go, from their manner, where the tumbrel awaited them. The clerk sprang ahead and opened the door. He bowed as they swept by him.

The girls went on along the Avenue and disdain was still on their faces.

'Honestly!' Annabel said. 'Can you imagine a thing like that?'

'Two hundred and fifty thousand dollars!' Midge said. 'That's a quarter of a million dollars right there!'

'He's got his nerve!' Annabel said.

They walked on. Slowly the disdain went, slowly and completely as if drained from them, and with it went the regal carriage and tread. Their shoulders dropped and they dragged their feet; they bumped against each other, without notice or apology, and caromed away again. They were silent and their eyes were cloudy.

Suddenly Midge straightened her back, flung her head high, and spoke, clear and strong.

'Listen, Annabel,' she said. 'Look. Suppose there was this terribly rich person, see? You don't know this person, but this person has seen you somewhere and wants to do something for you. Well, it's a terribly old person, see? And so this person dies, just like going to sleep, and leaves you ten million dollars. Now, what would be the first thing you'd do?'

You Were Perfectly Fine

The pale young man eased himself carefully into the low chair, and rolled his head to the side, so that the cool chintz comforted his cheek and temple.

'Oh, dear,' he said. 'Oh, dear, oh, dear, oh, dear. Oh.'

The clear-eyed girl, sitting light and erect on the couch, smiled brightly at him.

'Not feeling so well today?' she said.

'Oh, I'm great,' he said. 'Corking, I am. Know what time I got up? Four o'clock this afternoon, sharp. I kept trying to make it, and every time I took my head off the pillow, it would roll under the bed. This isn't my head I've got on now. I think this is something that used to belong to Walt Whitman. Oh, dear, oh, dear, oh, dear.'

'Do you think maybe a drink would make you feel better?' she said.

'The hair of the mastiff that bit me?' he said. 'Oh, no, thank you. Please never speak of anything like that again. I'm through. I'm all, all through. Look at that hand; steady as a humming-bird. Tell me, was I very terrible last night?'

'Oh, goodness,' she said, 'everybody was feeling pretty high. You were all right.'

'Yeah,' he said. 'I must have been dandy. Is everybody sore at me?'

'Good heavens, no,' she said. 'Everyone thought you were terribly funny. Of course, Jim Pierson was a little stuffy, there for a minute at dinner. But people sort of held him back in his chair, and got him calmed down. I don't think anybody at the other tables noticed it at all. Hardly anybody.'

'He was going to sock me?' he said. 'Oh, Lord. What did I do to him?'

'Why, you didn't do a thing,' she said. 'You were perfectly fine. But you know how silly Jim gets, when he thinks anybody is making too much fuss over Elinor.'

'Was I making a pass at Elinor?' he said. 'Did I do that?'

'Of course you didn't,' she said. 'You were only fooling, that's all. She thought you were awfully amusing. She was having a marvelous time. She only got a little tiny bit annoyed just once, when you poured the clam-juice down her back.'

'My God,' he said. 'Clam-juice down that back. And every vertebra a little Cabot. Dear God. What'll I ever do?'

'Oh, she'll be all right,' she said. 'Just send her some flowers, or something. Don't worry about it. It isn't anything.'

'No, I won't worry,' he said. 'I haven't got a care in the world. I'm sitting pretty. Oh, dear, oh, dear. Did I do any other fascinating tricks at dinner?'

'You were fine,' she said. 'Don't be so foolish about it. Everybody was crazy about you. The maître d'hôtel was a little worried because you wouldn't stop singing, but he really didn't mind. All he said was, he was afraid they'd close the place again, if there was so much noise. But he didn't care a bit, himself. I think he loved seeing you have such a good time. Oh, you were just singing away, there, for about an hour. It wasn't so terribly loud, at all.'

'So I sang,' he said. 'That must have been a treat. I sang.'

'Don't you remember?' she said. 'You just sang one song after another. Everybody in the place was listening. They loved it. Only you kept insisting that you wanted to sing some song about some kind of fusiliers or other, and everybody kept shushing you, and you'd keep trying to start it again. You were wonderful. We were all trying to make you stop singing for a minute, and eat something, but you wouldn't hear of it. My, you were funny.'

'Didn't I eat any dinner?' he said.

'Oh, not a thing,' she said. 'Every time the waiter would offer you something, you'd give it right back to him, because you said that he was your long-lost brother, changed in the cradle by a gypsy band, and that anything you had was his. You had him simply roaring at you.'

'I bet I did,' he said. 'I bet I was comical. Society's Pet, I must have been. And what happened then, after my overwhelming success with the waiter?'

'Why, nothing much,' she said. 'You took a sort of

dislike to some old man with white hair, sitting across the room, because you didn't like his necktie and you wanted to tell him about it. But we got you out, before he got really mad.'

'Oh, we got out,' he said. 'Did I walk?'

'Walk! Of course you did,' she said. 'You were absolutely all right. There was that nasty stretch of ice on the sidewalk, and you did sit down awfully hard, you poor dear. But good heavens, that might have happened to anybody.'

'Oh, sure,' he said. 'Louisa Alcott or anybody. So I fell down on the sidewalk. That would explain what's the matter with my – Yes. I see. And then what, if you don't mind?'

'Ah, now, Peter!' she said. 'You can't sit there and say you don't remember what happened after that! I did think that maybe you were just a little tight at dinner – oh, you were perfectly all right, and all that, but I did know you were feeling pretty gay. But you were so serious, from the time you fell down – I never knew you to be that way. Don't you know, how you told me I had never seen your real self before? Oh, Peter, I just couldn't bear it, if you didn't remember that lovely long ride we took together in the taxi! Please, you do remember that, don't you? I think it would simply kill me, if you didn't.'

'Oh, yes,' he said. 'Riding in the taxi. Oh, yes, sure. Pretty long ride, hmm?'

'Round and round and round the park,' she said. 'Oh,

and the trees were shining so in the moonlight. And you said you never knew before that you really had a soul.'

'Yes,' he said. 'I said that. That was me.'

'You said such lovely, lovely things,' she said. 'And I'd never known, all this time, how you had been feeling about me, and I'd never dared to let you see how I felt about you. And then last night – oh, Peter dear, I think that taxi ride was the most important thing that ever happened to us in our lives.'

'Yes,' he said. 'I guess it must have been.'

'And we're going to be so happy,' she said. 'Oh, I just want to tell everybody! But I don't know – I think maybe it would be sweeter to keep it all to ourselves.'

'I think it would be,' he said.

'Isn't it lovely?' she said.

'Yes,' he said. 'Great.'

'Lovely!' she said.

'Look here,' he said, 'do you mind if I have a drink? I mean, just medicinally, you know. I'm off the stuff for life, so help me. But I think I feel a collapse coming on.'

'Oh, I think it would do you good,' she said. 'You poor boy, it's a shame you feel so awful. I'll go make you a whisky and soda.'

'Honestly,' he said, 'I don't see how you could ever want to speak to me again, after I made such a fool of myself, last night. I think I'd better go join a monastery in Tibet.'

'You crazy idiot!' she said. 'As if I could ever let you

go away now! Stop talking like that. You were perfectly fine.'

She jumped up from the couch, kissed him quickly on the forehead, and ran out of the room.

The pale young man looked after her and shook his head long and slowly, then dropped it in his damp and trembling hands.

'Oh, dear,' he said. 'Oh, dear, oh, dear, oh, dear.'

Such a Pretty Little Picture

Mr Wheelock was clipping the hedge. He did not dislike doing it. If it had not been for the faintly sickish odor of the privet bloom, he would definitely have enjoyed it. The new shears were so sharp and bright, there was such a gratifying sense of something done as the young green stems snapped off and the expanse of tidy, square hedge-top lengthened. There was a lot of work to be done on it. It should have been attended to a week ago, but this was the first day that Mr Wheelock had been able to get back from the city before dinnertime.

Clipping the hedge was one of the few domestic duties that Mr Wheelock could be trusted with. He was notoriously poor at doing anything around the house. All the suburb knew about it. It was the source of all Mrs Wheelock's jokes. Her most popular anecdote was of how, the past winter, he had gone out and hired a man to take care of the furnace, after a seven-years' losing struggle with it. She had an admirable memory, and often as she had related the story, she never dropped a word of it. Even now, in the late summer, she could hardly tell it for laughing.

When they were first married, Mr Wheelock had lent himself to the fun. He had even posed as being more inefficient than he really was, to make the joke better. But he had tired of his helplessness, as a topic of conversation. All the men of Mrs Wheelock's acquaintance, her cousins, her brother-in-law, the boys she went to high school with, the neighbors' husbands, were adepts at putting up a shelf, at repairing a lock, or making a shirtwaist box. Mr Wheelock had begun to feel that there was something rather effeminate about his lack of interest in such things.

He had wanted to answer his wife, lately, when she enlivened some neighbor's dinner table with tales of his inadequacy with hammer and wrench. He had wanted to cry, 'All right, suppose I'm not any good at things like that. What of it?'

He had played with the idea, had tried to imagine how his voice would sound, uttering the words. But he could think of no further argument for his case than that 'What of it?' And he was a little relieved, somehow, at being able to find nothing stronger. It made it reassuringly impossible to go through with the plan of answering his wife's public railleries.

Mrs Wheelock sat, now, on the spotless porch of the neat stucco house. Beside her was a pile of her husband's shirts and drawers, the price-tags still on them. She was going over all the buttons before he wore the garments, sewing them on more firmly. Mrs Wheelock never waited for a button to come off, before sewing it on. She worked with quick, decided movements, compressing her lips each time the thread made a slight resistance to her deft jerks.

She was not a tall woman, and since the birth of her child she had gone over from a delicate plumpness to a settled stockiness. Her brown hair, though abundant, grew in an uncertain line about her forehead. It was her habit to put it up in curlers at night, but the crimps never came out in the right place. It was arranged with perfect neatness, yet it suggested that it had been done up and got over with as quickly as possible. Passionately clean, she was always redolent of the germicidal soap she used so vigorously. She was wont to tell people, somewhat redundantly, that she never employed any sort of cosmetics. She had unlimited contempt for women who sought to reduce their weight by dieting, cutting from their menus such nourishing items as cream and puddings and cereals.

Adelaide Wheelock's friends – and she had many of them – said of her that there was no nonsense about her. They and she regarded it as a compliment.

Sister, the Wheelocks' five-year-old daughter, played quietly in the gravel path that divided the tiny lawn. She had been known as Sister since her birth, and her mother still laid plans for a brother for her. Sister's baby carriage stood waiting in the cellar, her baby clothes were stacked expectantly away in bureau drawers. But raises were infrequent at the advertising agency where Mr Wheelock was employed, and his present salary had barely caught up to the cost of their living. They could not conscientiously regard themselves as being able to afford a son. Both Mr and Mrs Wheelock keenly felt his guilt in keeping the bassinet empty.

Sister was not a pretty child, though her features were straight, and her eyes would one day be handsome. The left one turned slightly in toward the nose, now, when she looked in a certain direction; they would operate as soon as she was seven. Her hair was pale and limp, and her color bad. She was a delicate little girl. Not fragile in a picturesque way, but the kind of child that must be always undergoing treatment for its teeth and its throat and obscure things in its nose. She had lately had her adenoids removed, and she was still using squares of surgical gauze instead of handkerchiefs. Both she and her mother somehow felt that these gave her a sort of prestige.

She was additionally handicapped by her frocks, which her mother bought a size or so too large, with a view to Sister's growing into them – an expectation which seemed never to be realized, for her skirts were always too long, and the shoulders of her little dresses came halfway down to her thin elbows. Yet, even discounting the unfortunate way she was dressed, you could tell, in some way, that she was never going to wear any kind of clothes well.

Mr Wheelock glanced at her now and then as he

clipped. He had never felt any fierce thrills of father-love for the child. He had been disappointed in her when she was a pale, large-headed baby, smelling of stale milk and warm rubber. Sister made him feel ill at ease, vaguely irritated him. He had had no share in her training; Mrs Wheelock was so competent a parent that she took the places of both of them. When Sister came to him to ask his permission to do something, he always told her to wait and ask her mother about it.

He regarded himself as having the usual paternal affection for his daughter. There were times, indeed, when she had tugged sharply at his heart – when he had waited in the corridor outside the operating room; when she was still under the anesthetic, and lay little and white and helpless on her high hospital bed; once when he had accidentally closed a door upon her thumb. But from the first he had nearly acknowledged to himself that he did not like Sister as a person.

Sister was not a whining child, despite her poor health. She had always been sensible and well-mannered, amenable about talking to visitors, rigorously unselfish. She never got into trouble, like other children. She did not care much for other children. She had heard herself described as being 'old-fashioned,' and she knew she was delicate, and she felt that these attributes rather set her above them. Besides, they were rough and careless of their bodily well-being.

Sister was exquisitely cautious of her safety. Grass, she

knew, was often apt to be damp in the late afternoon, so she was careful now to stay right in the middle of the gravel path, sitting on a folded newspaper and playing one of her mysterious games with three petunias that she had been allowed to pick. Mrs Wheelock never had to speak to her twice about keeping off wet grass, or wearing her rubbers, or putting on her jacket if a breeze sprang up. Sister was an immediately obedient child, always.

II

Mrs Wheelock looked up from her sewing and spoke to her husband. Her voice was high and clear, resolutely good-humored. From her habit of calling instructions from her upstairs window to Sister playing on the porch below, she spoke always a little louder than was necessary.

'Daddy,' she said.

She had called him Daddy since some eight months before Sister was born. She and the child had the same trick of calling his name and then waiting until he signified that he was attending before they went on with what they wanted to say.

Mr Wheelock stopped clipping, straightened himself and turned toward her.

'Daddy,' she went on, thus reassured, 'I saw Mr Ince down at the post office today when Sister and I went down to get the ten o'clock mail – there wasn't much, just a card for me from Grace Williams from that place they go to up on Cape Cod, and an advertisement from some department store or other about their summer fur sale (as if I cared!), and a circular for you from the bank. I opened it; I knew you wouldn't mind.

'Anyway, I just thought I'd tackle Mr Ince first as last about getting in our cordwood. He didn't see me at first – though I'll bet he really saw me and pretended not to – but I ran right after him. "Oh, Mr Ince!" I said. "Why, hello, Mrs Wheelock," he said, and then he asked for you, and I told him you were finely, and everything. Then I said, "Now, Mr Ince," I said, "how about getting in that cordwood of ours?" And he said, "Well, Mrs Wheelock," he said, "I'll get it in soon's I can, but I'm short of help right now," he said.

'Short of help! Of course I couldn't say anything, but I guess he could tell from the way I looked at him how much I believed it. I just said, "All right, Mr Ince, but don't you forget us. There may be a cold snap coming on," I said, "and we'll be wanting a fire in the living-room. Don't you forget us," I said, and he said, no, he wouldn't.

'If that wood isn't here by Monday, I think you ought to do something about it, Daddy. There's no sense in all this putting it off, and putting it off. First thing you know there'll be a cold snap coming on, and we'll be wanting a fire in the living-room, and there we'll be! You'll be sure and 'tend to it, won't you, Daddy? I'll remind you again Monday, if I can think of it, but there are so many things!'

Mr Wheelock nodded and turned back to his clipping – and his thoughts. They were thoughts that had occupied much of his leisure lately. After dinner, when Adelaide was sewing or arguing with the maid, he found himself letting his magazine fall face downward on his knee, while he rolled the same idea round and round in his mind. He had got so that he looked forward, through the day, to losing himself in it. He had rather welcomed the hedge-clipping; you can clip and think at the same time.

It had started with a story that he had picked up somewhere. He couldn't recall whether he had heard it or had read it – that was probably it, he thought, he had run across it in the back pages of some comic paper that someone had left on the train.

It was about a man who lived in a suburb. Every morning he had gone to the city on the 8:12, sitting in the same seat in the same car, and every evening he had gone home to his wife on the 5:17, sitting in the same seat in the same car. He had done this for twenty years of his life. And then one night he didn't come home. He never went back to his office any more. He just never turned up again.

The last man to see him was the conductor on the 5:17.

'He come down the platform at the Grand Central,' the man reported, 'just like he done every night since I been working on this road. He put one foot on the step,

23

and then he stopped sudden, and he said "Oh, hell," and he took his foot off of the step and walked away. And that's the last anybody see of him.'

Curious how that story took hold of Mr Wheelock's fancy. He had started thinking of it as a mildly humorous anecdote; he had come to accept it as fact. He did not think the man's sitting in the same seat in the same car need have been stressed so much. That seemed unimportant. He thought long about the man's wife, wondered what suburb he had lived in. He loved to play with the thing, to try to feel what the man felt before he took his foot off the car's step. He never concerned himself with speculations as to where the man had disappeared, how he had spent the rest of his life. Mr Wheelock was absorbed in that moment when he had said 'Oh, hell,' and walked off. 'Oh, hell' seemed to Mr Wheelock a fine thing for him to have said, a perfect summary of the situation.

He tried thinking of himself in the man's place. But no, he would have done it from the other end. That was the real way to do it.

Some summer evening like this, say, when Adelaide was sewing on buttons, up on the porch, and Sister was playing somewhere about. A pleasant, quiet evening it must be, with the shadows lying long on the street that led from their house to the station. He would put down the garden shears, or the hose, or whatever he happened to be puttering with – not throw the thing down, you know, just put it quietly aside – and walk out of the gate and down the street, and that would be the last they'd see of him. He would time it so that he'd just make the 6:03 for the city comfortably.

He did not go ahead with it from there, much. He was not especially anxious to leave the advertising agency forever. He did not particularly dislike his work. He had been an advertising solicitor since he had gone to work at all, and he worked hard at his job and, aside from that, didn't think about it much one way or the other.

It seemed to Mr Wheelock that before he had got hold of the 'Oh, hell' story he had never thought about anything much, one way or the other. But he would have to disappear from the office, too, that was certain. It would spoil everything to turn up there again. He thought dimly of taking a train going West, after the 6:03 got him to the Grand Central Terminal – he might go to Buffalo, say, or perhaps Chicago. Better just let that part take care of itself and go back to dwell on the moment when it would sweep over him that he was going to do it, when he would put down the shears and walk out the gate –

The 'Oh, hell' rather troubled him. Mr Wheelock felt that he would like to retain that; it completed the gesture so beautifully. But he didn't quite know to whom he should say it.

He might stop in at the post office on his way to the station and say it to the postmaster; but the postmaster would probably think he was only annoyed at there being no mail for him. Nor would the conductor of the 6:03, a train Mr Wheelock never used, take the right interest in it. Of course the real thing to do would be to say it to Adelaide just before he laid down the shears. But somehow Mr Wheelock could not make that scene come very clear in his imagination.

III

'Daddy,' Mrs Wheelock said briskly.

He stopped clipping, and faced her.

'Daddy,' she related, 'I saw Doctor Mann's automobile going by the house this morning – he was going to have a look at Mr Warren, his rheumatism's getting along nicely – and I called him in a minute, to look us over.'

She screwed up her face, winked, and nodded vehemently several times in the direction of the absorbed Sister, to indicate that she was the subject of the discourse.

'He said we were going ahead finely,' she resumed, when she was sure that he had caught the idea. 'Said there was no need for those t-o-n-s-i-l-s to c-o-m-e o-u-t. But I thought, soon's it gets a little cooler, some time next month, we'd just run in to the city and let Doctor Sturges have a look at us. I'd rather be on the safe side.'

'But Doctor Lytton said it wasn't necessary, and those doctors at the hospital, and now Doctor Mann, that's known her since she was a baby,' suggested Mr Wheelock.

'I know, I know,' replied his wife. 'But I'd rather be on the safe side.'

Mr Wheelock went back to his hedge.

Oh, of course he couldn't do it; he never seriously thought he could, for a minute. Of course he couldn't. He wouldn't have the shadow of an excuse for doing it. Adelaide was a sterling woman, an utterly faithful wife, an almost slavish mother. She ran his house economically and efficiently. She harried the suburban trades people into giving them dependable service, drilled the succession of poorly paid, poorly trained maids, cheerfully did the thousand fussy little things that go with the running of a house. She looked after his clothes, gave him medicine when she thought he needed it, oversaw the preparation of every meal that was set before him; they were not especially inspirational meals, but the food was always nourishing and, as a general thing, fairly well cooked. She never lost her temper, she was never depressed, never ill.

Not the shadow of an excuse. People would know that, and so they would invent an excuse for him. They would say there must be another woman.

Mr Wheelock frowned, and snipped at an obstinate young twig. Good Lord, the last thing he wanted was another woman. What he wanted was that moment when he realized he could do it, when he would lay down the shears –

Oh, of course he couldn't; he knew that as well as

anybody. What would they do, Adelaide and Sister? The house wasn't even paid for yet, and there would be that operation on Sister's eye in a couple of years. But the house would be all paid up by next March. And there was always that well-to-do brother-in-law of Adelaide's, the one who, for all his means, put up every shelf in that great big house with his own hands.

Decent people didn't just go away and leave their wives and families that way. All right, suppose you weren't decent; what of it? Here was Adelaide planning what she was going to do when it got a little cooler, next month. She was always planning ahead, always confident that things would go on just the same. Naturally, Mr Wheelock realized that he couldn't do it, as well as the next one. But there was no harm in fooling around with the idea. Would you say the 'Oh, hell' now, before you laid down the shears, or right after? How would it be to turn at the gate and say it?

Mr and Mrs Fred Coles came down the street arm-in-arm, from their neat stucco house on the corner.

'See they've got you working hard, eh?' cried Mr Coles genially, as they paused abreast of the hedge.

Mr Wheelock laughed politely, marking time for an answer.

'That's right,' he evolved.

Mrs Wheelock looked up from her work, shading her eyes with her thimbled hand against the long rays of the low sun.

'Yes, we finally got Daddy to do a little work,' she called brightly. 'But Sister and I are staying right here to watch over him, for fear he might cut his little self with the shears.'

There was general laughter, in which Sister joined. She had risen punctiliously at the approach of the older people, and she was looking politely at their eyes, as she had been taught.

'And how is my great big girl?' asked Mrs Coles, gazing fondly at the child.

'Oh, much better,' Mrs Wheelock answered for her. 'Doctor Mann says we are going ahead finely. I saw his automobile passing the house this morning – he was going to see Mr Warren, his rheumatism's coming along nicely – and I called him in a minute to look us over.'

She did the wink and the nods, at Sister's back. Mr and Mrs Coles nodded shrewdly back at her.

'He said there's no need for those t-o-n-s-i-l-s to c-o-m-e o-u-t,' Mrs Wheelock called. 'But I thought, soon's it gets a little cooler, some time next month, we'd just run in to the city and let Doctor Sturges have a look at us. I was telling Daddy, "I'd rather be on the safe side," I said.'

'Yes, it's better to be on the safe side,' agreed Mrs Coles, and her husband nodded again, sagely this time. She took his arm, and they moved slowly off.

'Been a lovely day, hasn't it?' she said over her shoulder, fearful of having left too abruptly. 'Fred and I are taking a little constitutional before supper.'

'Oh, taking a little constitutional?' cried Mrs Wheelock, laughing.

Mrs Coles laughed also, three or four bars.

'Yes, just taking a little constitutional before supper,' she called back.

Sister, weary of her game, mounted the porch, whimpering a little. Mrs Wheelock put aside her sewing, and took the tired child in her lap. The sun's last rays touched her brown hair, making it a shimmering gold. Her small, sharp face, the thick lines of her figure were in shadow as she bent over the little girl. Sister's head was hidden on her mother's shoulder, the folds of her rumpled white frock followed her limp, relaxed little body.

The lovely light was kind to the cheap, hurriedly built stucco house, to the clean gravel path, and the bits of closely cut lawn. It was gracious, too, to Mr Wheelock's tall, lean figure as he bent to work on the last few inches of unclipped hedge.

Twenty years, he thought. The man in the story went through with it for twenty years. He must have been a man along around forty-five, most likely. Mr Wheelock was thirty-seven. Eight years. It's a long time, eight years is. You could easily get so you could say that final 'Oh, hell,' even to Adelaide, in eight years. It probably wouldn't take more than four for you to know that you could do it. No, not more than two . . .

Mrs Coles paused at the corner of the street and looked back at the Wheelocks' house. The last of the light lingered on the mother and child group on the porch, gently touched the tall, white-clad figure of the husband and father as he went up to them, his work done.

Mrs Coles was a large, soft woman, barren, and addicted to sentiment.

'Look, Fred; just turn around and look at that,' she said to her husband. She looked again, sighing luxuriously. 'Such a pretty little picture!'

Glory in the Daytime

Mr Murdock was one who carried no enthusiasm whatever for plays and their players, and that was too bad, for they meant so much to little Mrs Murdock. Always she had been in a state of devout excitement over the luminous, free, passionate elect who serve the theater. And always she had done her wistful worshiping, along with the multitudes, at the great public altars. It is true that once, when she was a particularly little girl, love had impelled her to write Miss Maude Adams a letter beginning 'Dearest Peter,' and she had received from Miss Adams a miniature thimble inscribed 'A kiss from Peter Pan.' (That was a day!) And once, when her mother had taken her holiday shopping, a limousine door was held open and there had passed her, as close as *that,* a wonder of sable and violets and round red curls that seemed to tinkle on the air; so, forever after, she was as good as certain that she had been not a foot away from Miss Billie Burke. But until some three years after her marriage, these had remained her only personal experiences with the people of the lights and the glory.

Then it turned out that Miss Noyes, new come to little

Mrs Murdock's own bridge club, knew an actress. She actually knew an actress; the way you and I knew collectors of recipes and members of garden clubs and amateurs of needlepoint.

The name of the actress was Lily Wynton, and it was famous. She was tall and slow and silvery; often she appeared in the role of a duchess, or of a Lady Pam or an Honorable Moira. Critics recurrently referred to her as 'that great lady of our stage.' Mrs Murdock had attended, over years, matinee performances of the Wynton successes. And she had no more thought that she would one day have opportunity to meet Lily Wynton face to face than she had thought – well, than she had thought of flying!

Yet it was not astounding that Miss Noyes should walk at ease among the glamorous. Miss Noyes was full of depths and mystery, and she could talk with a cigarette still between her lips. She was always doing something difficult, like designing her own pajamas, or reading Proust, or modeling torsos in plasticine. She played excellent bridge. She liked little Mrs Murdock. 'Tiny one,' she called her.

'How's for coming to tea tomorrow, tiny one? Lily Wynton's going to drop up,' she said, at a therefore memorable meeting of the bridge club. 'You might like to meet her.'

The words fell so easily that she could not have realized their weight. Lily Wynton was coming to tea. Mrs Murdock might like to meet her. Little Mrs Murdock walked home through the early dark, and stars sang in the sky above her.

Mr Murdock was already at home when she arrived. It required but a glance to tell that for him there had been no singing stars that evening in the heavens. He sat with his newspaper opened at the financial page, and bitterness had its way with his soul. It was not the time to cry happily to him of the impending hospitalities of Miss Noyes; not the time, that is, if one anticipated exclamatory sympathy. Mr Murdock did not like Miss Noyes. When pressed for a reason, he replied that he just plain didn't like her. Occasionally he added, with a sweep that might have commanded a certain admiration, that all those women made him sick. Usually, when she told him of the temperate activities of the bridge club meetings, Mrs Murdock kept any mention of Miss Noyes's name from the accounts. She had found that this omission made for a more agreeable evening. But now she was caught in such a sparkling swirl of excitement that she had scarcely kissed him before she was off on her story.

'Oh, Jim,' she cried. 'Oh, what do you think! Hallie Noyes asked me to tea tomorrow to meet Lily Wynton!'

'Who's Lily Wynton?' he said.

'Ah, Jim,' she said. 'Ah, really, Jim. Who's Lily Wynton! Who's Greta Garbo, I suppose!'

'She some actress or something?' he said.

Mrs Murdock's shoulders sagged. 'Yes, Jim,' she said. 'Yes. Lily Wynton's an actress.'

She picked up her purse and started slowly toward the door. But before she had taken three steps, she was again caught up in her sparkling swirl. She turned to him, and her eyes were shining.

'Honestly,' she said, 'it was the funniest thing you ever heard in your life. We'd just finished the last rubber – oh, I forgot to tell you, I won three dollars, isn't that pretty good for me? – and Hallie Noyes said to me, "Come on in to tea tomorrow. Lily Wynton's going to drop up," she said. Just like that, she said it. Just as if it was anybody.'

'Drop up?' he said. 'How can you drop *up*?'

'Honestly, I don't know what I said when she asked me,' Mrs Murdock said. 'I suppose I said I'd love to – I guess I must have. But I was so simply – Well, you know how I've always felt about Lily Wynton. Why, when I was a little girl, I used to collect her pictures. And I've seen her in, oh, everything she's ever been in, I should think, and I've read every word about her, and interviews and all. Really and truly, when I think of *meeting* her – Oh, I'll simply die. What on earth shall I say to her?'

'You might ask her how she'd like to try dropping down, for a change,' Mr Murdock said.

'All right, Jim,' Mrs Murdock said. 'If that's the way you want to be.'

Wearily she went toward the door, and this time she reached it before she turned to him. There were no lights in her eyes.

'It – it isn't so awfully nice,' she said, 'to spoil

somebody's pleasure in something. I was so thrilled about this. You don't see what it is to me, to meet Lily Wynton. To meet somebody like that, and see what they're like, and hear what they say, and maybe get to know them. People like that mean – well, they mean something different to me. They're not like this. They're not like me. Who do I ever see? What do I ever hear? All my whole life, I've wanted to know – I've almost prayed that someday I could meet – Well. All right, Jim.'

She went out, and on to her bedroom.

Mr Murdock was left with only his newspaper and his bitterness for company. But he spoke aloud.

' "Drop up!" ' he said. ' "Drop *up*," for God's sake!'

The Murdocks dined, not in silence, but in pronounced quiet. There was something straitened about Mr Murdock's stillness; but little Mrs Murdock's was the sweet, far quiet of one given over to dreams. She had forgotten her weary words to her husband, she had passed through her excitement and her disappointment. Luxuriously she floated on innocent visions of days after the morrow. She heard her own voice in future conversations . . .

I saw Lily Wynton at Hallie's the other day, and she was telling me all about her new play – no, I'm terribly sorry, but it's a secret, I promised her I wouldn't tell anyone the name of it . . . Lily Wynton dropped up to tea yesterday, and we just got to talking, and she told me the most interesting things about her life; she said she'd never dreamed of telling them to anyone else . . . Why,

I'd love to come, but I promised to have lunch with Lily Wynton . . . I had a long, long letter from Lily Wynton . . . Lily Wynton called me up this morning . . . Whenever I feel blue, I just go and have a talk with Lily Wynton, and then I'm all right again . . . Lily Wynton told me . . . Lily Wynton and I . . . 'Lily,' I said to her . . .

The next morning, Mr Murdock had left for his office before Mrs Murdock rose. This had happened several times before, but not often. Mrs Murdock felt a little queer about it. Then she told herself that it was probably just as well. Then she forgot all about it, and gave her mind to the selection of a costume suitable to the afternoon's event. Deeply she felt that her small wardrobe included no dress adequate to the occasion; for, of course, such an occasion had never before arisen. She finally decided upon a frock of dark blue serge with fluted white muslin about the neck and wrists. It was her style, that was the most she could say for it. And that was all she could say for herself. Blue serge and little white ruffles – that was she.

The very becomingness of the dress lowered her spirits. A nobody's frock, worn by a nobody. She blushed and went hot when she recalled the dreams she had woven the night before, the mad visions of intimacy, of equality with Lily Wynton. Timidity turned her heart liquid, and she thought of telephoning Miss Noyes and saying she had a bad cold and could not come. She steadied, when she planned a course of conduct to pursue at teatime. She would not try to say anything; if she stayed silent, she could not sound foolish. She would listen and watch and worship and then come home, stronger, braver, better for an hour she would remember proudly all her life.

Miss Noyes's living-room was done in the early modern period. There were a great many oblique lines and acute angles, zigzags of aluminum and horizontal stretches of mirror. The color scheme was sawdust and steel. No seat was more than twelve inches above the floor, no table was made of wood. It was, as has been said of larger places, all right for a visit.

Little Mrs Murdock was the first arrival. She was glad of that; no, maybe it would have been better to have come after Lily Wynton; no, maybe this was right. The maid motioned her toward the living-room, and Miss Noyes greeted her in the cool voice and the warm words that were her special combination. She wore black velvet trousers, a red cummerbund, and a white silk shirt, opened at the throat. A cigarette clung to her lower lip, and her eyes, as was her habit, were held narrow against its near smoke.

'Come in, come in, tiny one,' she said. 'Bless its little heart. Take off its little coat. Good Lord, you look easily eleven years old in that dress. Sit ye doon, here beside of me. There'll be a spot of tea in a jiff.'

Mrs Murdock sat down on the vast, perilously low divan, and, because she was never good at reclining among cushions, held her back straight. There was room for six like her, between herself and her hostess. Miss Noyes lay back with one ankle flung upon the other knee, and looked at her.

'I'm a wreck,' Miss Noyes announced. 'I was modeling like a mad thing, all night long. It's taken everything out of me. I was like a thing bewitched.'

'Oh, what were you making?' cried Mrs Murdock.

'Oh, Eve,' Miss Noyes said. 'I always do Eve. What else is there to do? You must come pose for me some time, tiny one. You'd be nice to do. Ye-es, you'd be very nice to do. My tiny one.'

'Why, I –' Mrs Murdock said, and stopped. 'Thank you very much, though,' she said.

'I wonder where Lily is,' Miss Noyes said. 'She said she'd be here early – well, she always says that. You'll adore her, tiny one. She's really rare. She's a real person. And she's been through perfect hell. God, what a time she's had!'

'Ah, what's been the matter?' said Mrs Murdock.

'Men,' Miss Noyes said. 'Men. She never had a man that wasn't a louse.' Gloomily she stared at the toe of her flat-heeled patent leather pump. 'A pack of lice, always. All of them. Leave her for the first little floozie that comes along.'

'But –' Mrs Murdock began. No, she couldn't have heard right. How could it be right? Lily Wynton was a great actress. A great actress meant romance. Romance meant Grand Dukes and Crown Princes and diplomats

39

touched with gray at the temples and lean, bronzed, reckless Younger Sons. It meant pearls and emeralds and chinchilla and rubies red as the blood that was shed for them. It meant a grim-faced boy sitting in the fearful Indian midnight, beneath the dreary whirring of the *punkahs,* writing a letter to the lady he had seen but once; writing his poor heart out, before he turned to the service revolver that lay beside him on the table. It meant a golden-locked poet, floating face downward in the sea, and in his pocket his last great sonnet to the lady of ivory. It meant brave, beautiful men, living and dying for the lady who was the pale bride of art, whose eyes and heart were soft with only compassion for them.

A pack of lice. Crawling after little floozies; whom Mrs Murdock swiftly and hazily pictured as rather like ants.

'But –' said little Mrs Murdock.

'She gave them all her money,' Miss Noyes said. 'She always did. Or if she didn't, they took it anyway. Took every cent she had, and then spat in her face. Well, maybe I'm teaching her a little bit of sense now. Oh, there's the bell – that'll be Lily. No, sit ye doon, tiny one. You belong there.'

Miss Noyes rose and made for the archway that separated the living-room from the hall. As she passed Mrs Murdock, she stooped suddenly, cupped her guest's round chin, and quickly, lightly kissed her mouth.

'Don't tell Lily,' she murmured, very low.

Mrs Murdock puzzled. Don't tell Lily what? Could

Hallie Noyes think that she might babble to the Lily Wynton of these strange confidences about the actress's life? Or did she mean – But she had no more time for puzzling. Lily Wynton stood in the archway. There she stood, one hand resting on the wooden molding and her body swayed toward it, exactly as she stood for her third-act entrance of her latest play, and for a like half-minute.

You would have known her anywhere, Mrs Murdock thought. Oh, yes, anywhere. Or at least you would have exclaimed, 'That woman looks something like Lily Wynton.' For she was somehow different in the daylight. Her figure looked heavier, thicker, and her face – there was so much of her face that the surplus sagged from the strong, fine bones. And her eyes, those famous dark, liquid eyes. They were dark, yes, and certainly liquid, but they were set in little hammocks of folded flesh, and seemed to be set but loosely, so readily did they roll. Their whites, that were visible all around the irises, were threaded with tiny scarlet veins.

'I suppose footlights are an awful strain on their eyes,' thought little Mrs Murdock.

Lily Wynton wore, just as she should have, black satin and sables, and long white gloves were wrinkled luxuriously about her wrists. But there were delicate streaks of grime in the folds of her gloves, and down the shining length of her gown there were small, irregularly shaped dull patches; bits of food or drops of drink, or perhaps both, sometime must have slipped their carriers and found brief sanctuary there. Her hat – oh, her hat. It was romance, it was mystery, it was strange, sweet sorrow; it was Lily Wynton's hat, of all the world, and no other could dare it. Black it was, and tilted, and a great, soft plume drooped from it to follow her cheek and curl across her throat. Beneath it, her hair had the various hues of neglected brass. But, oh, her hat.

'Darling!' cried Miss Noyes.

'Angel,' said Lily Wynton. 'My sweet.'

It was that voice. It was that deep, soft, glowing voice. 'Like purple velvet,' someone had written. Mrs Murdock's heart beat visibly.

Lily Wynton cast herself upon the steep bosom of her hostess, and murmured there. Across Miss Noyes's shoulder she caught sight of little Mrs Murdock.

'And who is this?' she said. She disengaged herself.

'That's my tiny one,' Miss Noyes said. 'Mrs Murdock.'

'What a clever little face,' said Lily Wynton. 'Clever, clever little face. What does she do, sweet Hallie? I'm sure she writes, doesn't she? Yes, I can feel it. She writes beautiful, beautiful words. Don't you, child?'

'Oh, no, really I –' Mrs Murdock said.

'And you must write me a play,' said Lily Wynton. 'A beautiful, beautiful play. And I will play in it, over and over the world, until I am a very, very old lady. And then I will die. But I will never be forgotten, because of the years I played in your beautiful, beautiful play.'

She moved across the room. There was a slight

hesitancy, a seeming insecurity, in her step, and when she would have sunk into a chair, she began to sink two inches, perhaps, to its right. But she swayed just in time in her descent, and was safe.

'To write,' she said, smiling sadly at Mrs Murdock, 'to write. And such a little thing, for such a big gift. Oh, the privilege of it. But the anguish of it, too. The agony.'

'But, you see, I –' said little Mrs Murdock.

'Tiny one doesn't write, Lily,' Miss Noyes said. She threw herself back upon the divan. 'She's a museum piece. She's a devoted wife.'

'A wife!' Lily Wynton said. 'A wife. Your first marriage, child?'

'Oh, yes,' said Mrs Murdock.

'How sweet,' Lily Wynton said. 'How sweet, sweet, sweet. Tell me, child, do you love him very, very much?'

'Why, I –' said little Mrs Murdock, and blushed. 'I've been married for ages,' she said.

'You love him,' Lily Wynton said. 'You love him. And is it sweet to go to bed with him?'

'Oh –' said Mrs Murdock, and blushed till it hurt.

'The first marriage,' Lily Wynton said. 'Youth, youth. Yes, when I was your age I used to marry, too. Oh, treasure your love, child, guard it, live in it. Laugh and dance in the love of your man. Until you find out what he's really like.'

There came a sudden visitation upon her. Her shoulders jerked upward, her cheeks puffed, her eyes sought to start from their hammocks. For a moment she sat thus, then slowly all subsided into place. She lay back in her chair, tenderly patting her chest. She shook her head sadly, and there was grieved wonder in the look with which she held Mrs Murdock.

'Gas,' said Lily Wynton, in the famous voice. 'Gas. Nobody knows what I suffer from it.'

'Oh, I'm so sorry,' Mrs Murdock said. 'Is there anything –'

'Nothing,' Lily Wynton said. 'There is nothing. There is nothing that can be done for it. I've been everywhere.'

'How's for a spot of tea, perhaps?' Miss Noyes said. 'It might help.' She turned her face toward the archway and lifted up her voice. 'Mary! Where the hell's the tea?'

'You don't know,' Lily Wynton said, with her grieved eyes fixed on Mrs Murdock, 'you don't know what stomach distress is. You can never, never know, unless you're a stomach sufferer yourself. I've been one for years. Years and years and years.'

'I'm terribly sorry,' Mrs Murdock said.

'Nobody knows the anguish,' Lily Wynton said. 'The agony.'

The maid appeared, bearing a triangular tray upon which was set an heroic-sized tea service of bright white china, each piece a hectagon. She set it down on a table within the long reach of Miss Noyes and retired, as she had come, bashfully.

'Sweet Hallie,' Lily Wynton said, 'my sweet. Tea – I adore it. I worship it. But my distress turns it to gall and wormwood in me. Gall and wormwood. For hours, I should have no peace. Let me have a little, tiny bit of your beautiful, beautiful brandy, instead.'

'You really think you should, darling?' Miss Noyes said. 'You know –'

'My angel,' said Lily Wynton, 'it's the only thing for acidity.'

'Well,' Miss Noyes said. 'But do remember you've got a performance tonight.' Again she hurled her voice at the archway. 'Mary! Bring the brandy and a lot of soda and ice and things.'

'Oh, no, my saint,' Lily Wynton said. 'No, no, sweet Hallie. Soda and ice are rank poison to me. Do you want to freeze my poor, weak stomach? Do you want to kill poor, poor Lily?'

'Mary!' roared Miss Noyes. 'Just bring the brandy and a glass.' She turned to little Mrs Murdock. 'How's for your tea, tiny one? Cream? Lemon?'

'Cream, if I may, please,' Mrs Murdock said. 'And two lumps of sugar, please, if I may.'

'Oh, youth, youth,' Lily Wynton said. 'Youth and love.'

The maid returned with an octagonal tray supporting a decanter of brandy and a wide, squat, heavy glass. Her head twisted on her neck in a spasm of diffidence.

'Just pour it for me, will you, my dear?' said Lily

Wynton. 'Thank you. And leave the pretty, pretty decanter here, on this enchanting little table. Thank you. You're so good to me.'

The maid vanished, fluttering. Lily Wynton lay back in her chair, holding in her gloved hand the wide, squat glass, colored brown to the brim. Little Mrs Murdock lowered her eyes to her teacup, carefully carried it to her lips, sipped, and replaced it on its saucer. When she raised her eyes, Lily Wynton lay back in her chair, holding in her gloved hand the wide, squat, colorless glass.

'My life,' Lily Wynton said, slowly, 'is a mess. A stinking mess. It always has been, and it always will be. Until I am a very, very old lady. Ah, little Clever-Face, you writers don't know what struggle is.'

'But really I'm not –' said Mrs Murdock.

'To write,' Lily Wynton said. 'To write. To set one word beautifully beside another word. The privilege of it. The blessed, blessed peace of it. Oh, for quiet, for rest. But do you think those cheap bastards would close that play while it's doing a nickel's worth of business? Oh, no. Tired as I am, sick as I am, I must drag along. Oh, child, child, guard your precious gift. Give thanks for it. It is the greatest thing of all. It is the only thing. To write.'

'Darling, I told you tiny one doesn't write,' said Miss Noyes. 'How's for making more sense? She's a wife.'

'Ah, yes, she told me. She told me she had perfect, passionate love,' Lily Wynton said. 'Young love. It is the greatest thing. It is the only thing.' She grasped the decanter; and again the squat glass was brown to the brim.

'What time did you start today, darling?' said Miss Noyes.

'Oh, don't scold me, sweet love,' Lily Wynton said. 'Lily hasn't been naughty. Her wuzzunt naughty dirl 't all. I didn't get up until late, late, late. And though I parched, though I burned, I didn't have a drink until after my breakfast. "It is for Hallie," I said.' She raised the glass to her mouth, tilted it, and brought it away, colorless.

'Good Lord, Lily,' Miss Noyes said. 'Watch yourself. You've got to walk on that stage tonight, my girl.'

'All the world's a stage,' said Lily Wynton. 'And all the men and women merely players. They have their entrance and their exitses, and each man in his time plays many parts, his act being seven ages. At first, the infant, mewling and puking –'

'How's the play doing?' Miss Noyes said.

'Oh, lousily,' Lily Wynton said. 'Lousily, lousily, lousily. But what isn't? What isn't, in this terrible, terrible world? Answer me that.' She reached for the decanter.

'Lily, listen,' said Miss Noyes. 'Stop that. Do you hear?'

'Please, sweet Hallie,' Lily Wynton said. 'Pretty please. Poor, poor Lily.'

'Do you want me to do what I had to do last time?' Miss Noyes said. 'Do you want me to strike you, in front of tiny one, here?'

Lily Wynton drew herself high. 'You do not realize,' she said, icily, 'what acidity is.' She filled the glass and held it, regarding it as though through a lorgnon. Suddenly her manner changed, and she looked up and smiled at little Mrs Murdock.

'You must let me read it,' she said. 'You mustn't be so modest.'

'Read – ?' said little Mrs Murdock.

'Your play,' Lily Wynton said. 'Your beautiful, beautiful play. Don't think I am too busy. I always have time. I have time for everything. Oh, my God, I have to go to the dentist tomorrow. Oh, the suffering I have gone through with my teeth. Look!' She set down her glass, inserted a gloved forefinger in the corner of her mouth, and dragged it to the side. 'Oogh!' she insisted. 'Oogh!'

Mrs Murdock craned her neck shyly, and caught a glimpse of shining gold.

'Oh, I'm so sorry,' she said.

'As wah ee id a me ass ime,' Lily Wynton said. She took away her forefinger and let her mouth resume its shape. 'That's what he did to me last time,' she repeated. 'The anguish of it. The agony. Do you suffer with your teeth, little Clever-Face?'

'Why, I'm afraid I've been awfully lucky,' Mrs Murdock said. 'I –'

'You don't know,' Lily Wynton said. 'Nobody knows what it is. You writers – you don't know.' She took up her glass, sighed over it, and drained it.

'Well,' Miss Noyes said. 'Go ahead and pass out, then, darling. You'll have time for a sleep before the theater.'

'To sleep,' Lily Wynton said. 'To sleep, perchance to dream. The privilege of it. Oh, Hallie, sweet, sweet Hallie, poor Lily feels so terrible. Rub my head for me, angel. Help me.'

'I'll go get the Eau de Cologne,' Miss Noyes said. She left the room, lightly patting Mrs Murdock's knee as she passed her. Lily Wynton sat in her chair and closed her famous eyes.

'To sleep,' she said. 'To sleep, perchance to dream.'

'I'm afraid,' little Mrs Murdock began. 'I'm afraid,' she said, 'I really must be going home. I'm afraid I didn't realize how awfully late it was.'

'Yes, go, child,' Lily Wynton said. She did not open her eyes. 'Go to him. Go to him, live in him, love him. Stay with him always. But when he starts bringing them into the house – get out.'

'I'm afraid – I'm afraid I didn't quite understand,' Mrs Murdock said.

'When he starts bringing his fancy women into the house,' Lily Wynton said. 'You must have pride, then. You must go. I always did. But it was always too late then. They'd got all my money. That's all they want, marry them or not. They say it's love, but it isn't. Love is the only thing. Treasure your love, child. Go back to him. Go to bed with him. It's the only thing. And your beautiful, beautiful play.'

49

'Oh, dear,' said little Mrs Murdock. 'I – I'm afraid it's really terribly late.'

There was only the sound of rhythmic breathing from the chair where Lily Wynton lay. The purple voice rolled along the air no longer.

Little Mrs Murdock stole to the chair upon which she had left her coat. Carefully she smoothed her white muslin frills, so that they would be fresh beneath the jacket. She felt a tenderness for her frock; she wanted to protect it. Blue serge and little ruffles – they were her own.

When she reached the outer door of Miss Noyes's apartment, she stopped a moment and her manners conquered her. Bravely she called in the direction of Miss Noyes's bedroom.

'Good-by, Miss Noyes,' she said. 'I've simply got to run. I didn't realize it was so late. I had a lovely time – thank you ever so much.'

'Oh, good-by, tiny one,' Miss Noyes called. 'Sorry Lily went by-by. Don't mind her – she's really a real person. I'll call you up, tiny one. I want to see you. Now where's that damned Cologne?'

'Thank you ever so much,' Mrs Murdock said. She let herself out of the apartment.

Little Mrs Murdock walked homeward, through the clustering dark. Her mind was busy, but not with memories of Lily Wynton. She thought of Jim; Jim, who had left for his office before she had arisen that morning, Jim, whom she had not kissed good-by. Darling Jim. There were no others born like him. Funny Jim, stiff and cross and silent; but only because he knew so much. Only because he knew the silliness of seeking afar for the glamour and beauty and romance of living. When they were right at home all the time, she thought. Like the Blue Bird, thought little Mrs Murdock.

Darling Jim. Mrs Murdock turned in her course, and entered an enormous shop where the most delicate and esoteric of foods were sold for heavy sums. Jim liked red caviar. Mrs Murdock bought a jar of the shiny, glutinous eggs. They would have cocktails that night, though they had no guests, and the red caviar would be served with them for a surprise, and it would be a little, secret party to celebrate her return to contentment with her Jim, a party to mark her happy renunciation of all the glory of the world. She bought, too, a large, foreign cheese. It would give a needed touch to dinner. Mrs Murdock had not given much attention to ordering dinner, that morning. 'Oh, anything you want, Signe,' she had said to the maid. She did not want to think of that. She went on home with her packages.

Mr Murdock was already there when she arrived. He was sitting with his newspaper opened to the financial page. Little Mrs Murdock ran into him with her eyes a-light. It is too bad that the light in a person's eyes is only the light in a person's eyes, and you cannot tell at a look what causes it. You do not know if it is excitement about you, or about something else. The evening before, Mrs

Murdock had run in to Mr Murdock with her eyes a-light.

'Oh, hello,' he said to her. He looked back at this paper, and kept his eyes there. 'What did you do? Did you drop up to Hank Noyes's?'

Little Mrs Murdock stopped right where she was.

'You know perfectly well, Jim,' she said, 'that Hallie Noyes's first name is Hallie.'

'It's Hank to me,' he said. 'Hank or Bill. Did what's-her-name show up? I mean drop up. Pardon me.'

'To whom are you referring?' said Mrs Murdock, perfectly.

'What's-her-name,' Mr Murdock said. 'The movie star.'

'If you mean Lily Wynton,' Mrs Murdock said, 'she is not a movie star. She is an actress. She is a great actress.'

'Well, did she drop up?' he said.

Mrs Murdock's shoulders sagged. 'Yes,' she said. 'Yes, she was there, Jim.'

'I suppose you're going on the stage now,' he said.

'Ah, Jim,' Mrs Murdock said. 'Ah, Jim, please. I'm not sorry at all I went to Hallie Noyes's today. It was – it was a real experience to meet Lily Wynton. Something I'll remember all my life.'

'What did she do?' Mr Murdock said. 'Hang by her feet?'

'She did no such thing!' Mrs Murdock said. 'She recited Shakespeare, if you want to know.'

'Oh, my God,' Mr Murdock said. 'That must have been great.'

'All right, Jim,' Mrs Murdock said. 'If that's the way you want to be.'

Wearily she left the room and went down the hall. She stopped at the pantry door, pushed it open, and spoke to the pleasant little maid.

'Oh, Signe,' she said. 'Oh, good evening, Signe. Put these things somewhere, will you? I got them on the way home. I thought we might have them some time.'

Wearily little Mrs Murdock went on down the hall to her bedroom.

From the Diary of a New York Lady

During Days of Horror, Despair, and World Change

MONDAY. Breakfast tray about eleven; didn't want it. The champagne at the Amorys' last night was *too* revolting, but what *can* you do? You can't stay until five o'clock on just *nothing*. They had those *divine* Hungarian musicians in the green coats, and Stewie Hunter took off one of his shoes and led them with it, and it *couldn't* have been funnier. He is *the* wittiest number in the *entire* world; he *couldn't* be more perfect. Ollie Martin brought me home and we both fell asleep in the car – *too* screaming. Miss Rose came about noon to do my nails, simply *covered* with *the* most divine gossip. The Morrises are going to separate *any minute*, and Freddie Warren *definitely* has ulcers, and Gertie Leonard simply *won't* let Bill Crawford out of her sight even with Jack Leonard *right there in the room*, and it's all *true* about Sheila Phillips and Babs Deering. It *couldn't* have been more thrilling. Miss Rose is *too* marvelous; I really think that a lot of times people like that are a lot more intelligent than a lot of people. Didn't notice until after she had gone that the damn fool had put that *revolting* tangerine-colored polish on my nails; *couldn't* have been more furious. Started to read a book, but too nervous. Called up and found I could get two tickets for the opening of 'Run like a Rabbit' tonight for forty-eight dollars. Told them they had *the* nerve of the world, but what *can* you do? Think Joe said he was dining out, so telephoned some *divine* numbers to get someone to go to the theater with me, but they were all tied up. Finally got Ollie Martin. He *couldn't* have more poise, and what do *I* care if he *is* one? *Can't* decide whether to wear the green crepe or the red wool. Every time I look at my finger nails, I could *spit*. *Damn* Miss Rose.

TUESDAY. Joe came barging in my room this morning at *practically nine o'clock*. *Couldn't* have been more furious. Started to fight, but *too* dead. Know he said he wouldn't be home to dinner. Absolutely *cold* all day; couldn't *move*. Last night *couldn't* have been more perfect. Ollie and I dined at Thirty-Eight East, absolutely *poisonous* food, and not one *living* soul that you'd be seen *dead* with, and 'Run like a Rabbit' was *the* world's worst. Took Ollie up to the Barlows' party and it *couldn't* have been more attractive – *couldn't* have been more people absolutely *stinking*. They had those Hungarians in the green coats, and Stewie Hunter was leading them with a fork – everybody simply *died*. He had *yards* of green toilet paper hung around his neck like a lei; he *couldn't* have been in better form. Met a *really new number*, very tall, *too* marvelous, and one of those people that you can *really* talk to them. I told him sometimes I get so *nauseated* I could *yip*, and I felt I absolutely *had* to do something like write or paint. He said why didn't I write or paint. Came home alone; Ollie passed out *stiff*. Called up the new number three times today to get him to come to dinner and go with me to the opening of 'Never Say Good Morning,' but first he was out and then he was all tied up with his mother. Finally got Ollie Martin. Tried to read a book, but couldn't sit still. *Can't* decide whether to wear the red lace or the pink with the feathers. Feel *too* exhausted, but what *can* you do?

WEDNESDAY. The most terrible thing happened *just this minute*. Broke one of my finger nails *right off short*. Absolutely *the* most horrible thing I ever had happen to me in my life. Called up Miss Rose to come over and shape it for me, but she was out for the day. I do have *the* worst luck in the *entire* world. Now I'll have to go around like this all day and all night, but what *can* you do? *Damn* Miss Rose. Last night *too* hectic. 'Never Say Good Morning' *too* foul, *never* saw more poisonous clothes on the stage. Took Ollie up to the Ballards' party; *couldn't* have been better. They had those Hungarians in the green coats and Stewie Hunter was leading them with a freesia – *too* perfect. He had on Peggy Cooper's ermine coat and Phyllis Minton's silver turban; *simply* unbelievable. Asked simply *sheaves* of *divine* people to come here Friday night;

got the address of those Hungarians in the green coats
from Betty Ballard. She says just engage them until four,
and then whoever gives them another three hundred dollars, they'll stay till five. *Couldn't* be cheaper. Started home
with Ollie, but had to drop him at his house; he *couldn't*
have been sicker. Called up the new number today to get
him to come to dinner and go to the opening of 'Everybody Up' with me tonight, but he was tied up. Joe's going
to be out; he didn't *condescend* to say *where, of course.*
Started to read the papers, but nothing in them except
that Mona Wheatley is in Reno charging *intolerable cruelty.*
Called up Jim Wheatley to see if he had anything to do
tonight, but he was tied up. Finally got Ollie Martin.
Can't decide whether to wear the white satin or the black
chiffon or the yellow pebble crepe. Simply *wrecked* to the
core about my finger nail. Can't *bear* it. *Never* knew *anybody* to have such *unbelievable* things happen to them.

THURSDAY. Simply *collapsing* on my *feet.* Last night *too*
marvelous. 'Everybody Up' *too* divine, *couldn't* be filthier,
and the new number was there, *too* celestial, only he
didn't see me. He was with Florence Keeler in that *loath-
some* gold Schiaparelli model of hers that every *shop-girl*
has had since *God* knows. He must be out of his *mind*;
she wouldn't *look* at a man. Took Ollie to the Watsons'
party; *couldn't* have been more thrilling. Everybody
simply *blind.* They had those Hungarians in the green
coats and Stewie Hunter was leading them with a lamp,

and, after the lamp got broken, he and Tommy Thomas did adagio dances – *too* wonderful. Somebody told me Tommy's doctor told him he had to absolutely get *right out of town*, he has *the* world's worst stomach, but you'd *never* know it. Came home alone, couldn't find Ollie *anywhere*. Miss Rose came at noon to shape my nail, *couldn't* have been more fascinating. Sylvia Eaton can't go *out the door* unless she's had a hypodermic, and Doris Mason *knows every single word* about Douggie Mason and that girl up in Harlem, and Evelyn North won't be *induced* to keep away from those three acrobats, and they don't *dare* tell Stuyvie Raymond *what* he's got the matter with him. *Never* knew anyone that had a more simply *fascinating* life than Miss Rose. Made her take that *vile* tangerine polish off my nails and put on dark red. Didn't notice until after she had gone that it's practically *black* in electric light; *couldn't* be in a worse state. *Damn* Miss Rose. Joe left a note saying he was going to dine out, so telephoned the new number to get him to come to dinner and go with me to that new movie tonight, but he didn't answer. Sent him three telegrams to *absolutely surely* come tomorrow night. Finally got Ollie Martin for tonight. Looked at the papers, but nothing in them except that the Harry Motts are throwing a tea with Hungarian music on Sunday. Think will ask the new number to go to it with me; they must have meant to invite me. Began to read a book, but too exhausted. *Can't* decide whether to wear the new blue with the white jacket or save it till tomorrow night and wear the ivory moire. Simply *heartsick* every time I think of my nails. *Couldn't* be wilder. Could *kill* Miss Rose, but what *can* you do?

FRIDAY. Absolutely *sunk*; *couldn't* be worse. Last night *too* divine, movie *simply* deadly. Took Ollie to the Kingslands' party, *too* unbelievable, everybody absolutely *rolling*. They had those Hungarians in the green coats, but Stewie Hunter wasn't there. He's got a *complete* nervous breakdown. Worried *sick* for fear he won't be well by tonight; will absolutely *never* forgive him if he doesn't come. Started home with Ollie, but dropped him at his house because he *couldn't* stop crying. Joe left word with the butler he's going to the country this afternoon for the week-end; *of course* he wouldn't *stoop* to say *what* country. Called up *streams* of marvelous numbers to get someone to come dine and go with me to the opening of 'White Man's Folly,' and then go somewhere after to dance for a while; can't *bear* to be the first one there at your own party. Everybody was tied up. Finally got Ollie Martin. *Couldn't* feel more depressed; never should have gone *anywhere near* champagne and Scotch together. Started to read a book, but too restless. Called up Anne Lyman to ask about the new baby and *couldn't* remember if it was a boy or girl – *must* get a secretary *next week*. Anne *couldn't* have been more of a help; she said she didn't know whether to name it Patricia or Gloria, so then of course I knew it was a girl *right away*. Suggested calling it Barbara; forgot she already had one.

Absolutely *walking the floor* like a *panther* all day. Could *spit* about Stewie Hunter. Can't *face* deciding whether to wear the blue with the white jacket or the purple with the beige roses. Every time I look at those *revolting* black nails, I want to absolutely *yip*. I really have *the* most horrible things happen to me of anybody in the *entire* world. *Damn* Miss Rose.

Mr Durant

Not for some ten days had Mr Durant known any such ease of mind. He gave himself up to it, wrapped himself, warm and soft, as in a new and an expensive cloak. God, for Whom Mr Durant entertained a good-humored affection, was in His heaven, and all was again well with Mr Durant's world.

Curious how this renewed peace sharpened his enjoyment of the accustomed things about him. He looked back at the rubber works, which he had just left for the day, and nodded approvingly at the solid red pile, at the six neat stories rising impressively into the darkness. You would go far, he thought, before you would find a more up-and-coming outfit, and there welled in him a pleasing, proprietary sense of being a part of it.

He gazed amiably down Center Street, noting how restfully the lights glowed. Even the wet, dented pavement, spotted with thick puddles, fed his pleasure by reflecting the discreet radiance above it. And to complete his comfort, the car for which he was waiting, admirably on time, swung into view far down the track. He thought, with a sort of jovial tenderness, of what it would bear him to; of his dinner – it was fish-chowder night – of his children, of his wife, in the order named. Then he turned his kindly attention to the girl who stood near him, obviously awaiting the Center Street car, too. He was delighted to feel a sharp interest in her. He regarded it as being distinctly creditable to himself that he could take a healthy notice of such matters once more. Twenty years younger – that's what he felt.

Rather shabby, she was, in her rough coat with its shagginess rubbed off here and there. But there was a something in the way her cheaply smart turban was jammed over her eyes, in the way her thin young figure moved under the loose coat. Mr Durant pointed his tongue, and moved it delicately along his cool, smooth upper lip.

The car approached, clanged to a stop before them. Mr Durant stepped gallantly aside to let the girl get in first. He did not help her to enter, but the solicitous way in which he superintended the process gave all the effect of his having actually assisted her.

Her tight little skirt slipped up over her thin, pretty legs as she took the high step. There was a run in one of her flimsy silk stockings. She was doubtless unconscious of it; it was well back toward the seam, extending, probably from her garter, half-way down the calf. Mr Durant had an odd desire to catch his thumbnail in the present end of the run, and to draw it on down until the slim line of the dropped stitches reached to the top of her low shoe.

An indulgent smile at his whimsy played about his mouth, broadening to a grin of affable evening greeting for the conductor, as he entered the car and paid his fare.

The girl sat down somewhere far up at the front. Mr Durant found a desirable seat toward the rear, and craned his neck to see her. He could catch a glimpse of a fold of her turban and a bit of her brightly rouged cheek, but only at a cost of holding his head in a strained, and presently painful, position. So, warmed by the assurance that there would always be others, he let her go, and settled himself restfully. He had a ride of twenty minutes or so before him. He allowed his head to fall gently back, to let his eyelids droop, and gave himself to his thoughts. Now that the thing was comfortably over and done with, he could think of it easily, almost laughingly. Last week, now, and even part of the week before, he had had to try with all his strength to force it back every time it wrenched itself into his mind. It had positively affected his sleep. Even though he was shielded by his newly acquired amused attitude, Mr Durant felt indignation flood within him when he recalled those restless nights.

He had met Rose for the first time about three months before. She had been sent up to his office to take some letters for him. Mr Durant was assistant manager of the rubber company's credit department; his wife was wont to refer to him as one of the officers of the company, and, though she often spoke thus of him to people in his presence, he never troubled to go more fully into detail about

63

his position. He rated a room, a desk, and a telephone to himself; but not a stenographer. When he wanted to give dictation or to have some letters typewritten, he telephoned around to the various other offices until he found a girl who was not busy with her own work. That was how Rose had come to him.

She was not a pretty girl. Distinctly, no. But there was a rather sweet fragility about her, and an almost desperate timidity that Mr Durant had once found engaging, but that he now thought of with a prickling irritation. She was twenty, and the glamour of youth was around her. When she bent over her work, her back showing white through her sleazy blouse, her clean hair coiled smoothly on her thin neck, her straight, childish legs crossed at the knee to support her pad, she had an undeniable appeal.

But not pretty – no. Her hair wasn't the kind that went up well, her eyelashes and lips were too pale, she hadn't much knack about choosing and wearing her cheap clothes. Mr Durant, in reviewing the thing, felt a surprise that she should ever have attracted him. But it was a tolerant surprise, not an impatient one. Already he looked back on himself as being just a big boy in the whole affair.

It did not occur to him to feel even a flicker of astonishment that Rose should have responded so eagerly to him, an immovably married man of forty-nine. He never thought of himself in that way. He used to tell Rose, laughingly, that he was old enough to be her father, but neither of them ever really believed it. He regarded her

affection for him as the most natural thing in the world –
there she was, coming from a much smaller town, never
the sort of girl to have had admirers; naturally, she was
dazzled at the attentions of a man who, as Mr Durant put
it, was approaching the prime. He had been charmed with
the idea of there having been no other men in her life;
but lately, far from feeling flattered at being the first and
only one, he had come to regard it as her having taken a
sly advantage of him, to put him in that position.

It had all been surprisingly easy. Mr Durant knew it
would be almost from the first time he saw her. That did
not lessen its interest in his eyes. Obstacles discouraged
him, rather than led him on. Elimination of bother was
the main thing.

Rose was not a coquettish girl. She had that curious
directness that some very timid people possess. There
were her scruples, of course, but Mr Durant readily rea-
soned them away. Not that he was a master of technique,
either. He had had some experiences, probably a third as
many as he habitually thought of himself as having been
through, but none that taught him much of the delicate
shadings of wooing. But then, Rose's simplicity asked
exceedingly little.

She was never one to demand much of him, anyway.
She never thought of stirring up any trouble between him
and his wife, never besought him to leave his family and
go away with her, even for a day. Mr Durant valued her
for that. It did away with a lot of probable fussing.

It was amazing how free they were, how little lying there was to do. They stayed in the office after hours – Mr Durant found many letters that must be dictated. No one thought anything of that. Rose was busy most of the day, and it was only considerate that Mr Durant should not break in on her employer's time, only natural that he should want as good a stenographer as she was to attend to his correspondence.

Rose's only relative, a married sister, lived in another town. The girl roomed with an acquaintance named Ruby, also employed at the rubber works, and Ruby, who was much taken up with her own affairs of the emotions, never appeared to think it strange if Rose was late to dinner, or missed the meal entirely. Mr Durant readily explained to his wife that he was detained by a rush of business. It only increased his importance, to her, and spurred her on to devising especially pleasing dishes, and solicitously keeping them hot for his return. Sometimes, important in their guilt, Rose and he put out the light in the little office and locked the door, to trick the other employees into thinking that they had long ago gone home. But no one ever so much as rattled the doorknob, seeking admission.

It was all so simple that Mr Durant never thought of it as anything outside the usual order of things. His interest in Rose did not blunt his appreciation of chance attractive legs or provocative glances. It was an entanglement of the most restful, comfortable nature. It even held a sort of homelike quality, for him.

And then everything had to go and get spoiled. 'Wouldn't you know?' Mr Durant asked himself, with deep bitterness.

Ten days before, Rose had come weeping to his office. She had the sense to wait till after hours, for a wonder, but anybody might have walked in and seen her blubbering there; Mr Durant felt it to be due only to the efficient management of his personal God that no one had. She wept, as he sweepingly put it, all over the place. The color left her cheeks and collected damply in her nose, and rims of vivid pink grew around her pale eyelashes. Even her hair became affected; it came away from the pins, and stray ends of it wandered limply over her neck. Mr Durant hated to look at her, could not bring himself to touch her.

All his energies were expended in urging her for God's sake to keep quiet; he did not ask her what was the matter. But it came out, between bursts of unpleasant-sounding sobs. She was 'in trouble.' Neither then nor in the succeeding days did she and Mr Durant ever use any less delicate phrase to describe her condition. Even in their thoughts, they referred to it that way.

She had suspected it, she said, for some time, but she hadn't wanted to bother him about it until she was absolutely sure. 'Didn't want to bother me!' thought Mr Durant.

Naturally, he was furious. Innocence is a desirable thing, a dainty thing, an appealing thing, in its place; but carried too far, it is merely ridiculous. Mr Durant wished to God that he had never seen Rose. He explained this desire to her.

But that was no way to get things done. As he had often jovially remarked to his friends, he knew 'a thing or two.' Cases like this could be what people of the world called 'fixed up' – New York society women, he understood, thought virtually nothing of it. This case could be fixed up, too. He got Rose to go home, telling her not to worry, he would see that everything was all right. The main thing was to get her out of sight, with that nose and those eyes.

But knowing a thing or two and putting the knowledge into practice turned out to be vastly different things. Mr Durant did not know whom to seek for information. He pictured himself inquiring of his intimates if they could tell him of 'someone that this girl he had heard about could go to.' He could hear his voice uttering the words, could hear the nervous laugh that would accompany them, the terrible flatness of them as they left his lips. To confide in one person would be confiding in at least one too many. It was a progressing town, but still small enough for gossip to travel like a typhoon. Not that he thought for a moment that his wife would believe any such thing, if it reached her; but where would be the sense in troubling her?

Mr Durant grew pale and jumpy over the thing as the days went by. His wife worried herself into one of her sick spells over his petulant refusals of second helpings. There daily arose in him an increasing anger that he should be drawn into conniving to find a way to break the law of his country – probably the law of every country in the world. Certainly of every decent, Christian place.

It was Ruby, finally, who got them out of it. When Rose confessed to him that she had broken down and told Ruby, his rage leaped higher than any words. Ruby was secretary to the vice-president of the rubber company. It would be pretty, wouldn't it, if she let it out? He had lain wide-eyed beside his wife all that night through. He shuddered at the thought of chance meetings with Ruby in the hall.

But Ruby had made it delightfully simple, when they did meet. There were no reproachful looks, no cold turnings away of the head. She had given him her usual smiling 'good-morning,' and added a little upward glance, mischievous, understanding, with just the least hint of admiration in it. There was a sense of intimacy, of a shared secret binding them cozily together. A fine girl, that Ruby!

Ruby had managed it all without any fuss. Mr Durant was not directly concerned in the planning. He heard of it only through Rose, on the infrequent occasions when he had had to see her. Ruby knew, through some indistinct friends of hers, of 'a woman.' It would be twenty-five dollars. Mr Durant had gallantly insisted upon giving Rose the money. She had started to sniffle about taking it, but he had finally prevailed. Not that he couldn't have used the twenty-five very nicely himself, just then, with Junior's teeth, and all!

Well, it was all over now. The invaluable Ruby had gone with Rose to 'the woman'; had that very afternoon taken her to the station and put her on a train for her sister's. She had even thought of wiring the sister beforehand that Rose had had influenza and must have a rest.

Mr Durant had urged Rose to look on it as just a little vacation. He promised, moreover, to put in a good word for her whenever she wanted her job back. But Rose had gone pink about the nose again at the thought. She had sobbed her rasping sobs, then had raised her face from her stringy handkerchief and said, with an entirely foreign firmness, that she never wanted to see the rubber works or Ruby or Mr Durant again. He had laughed indulgently, had made himself pat her thin back. In his relief at the outcome of things, he could be generous to the pettish.

He chuckled inaudibly, as he reviewed that last scene. 'I suppose she thought she'd make me sore, saying she was never coming back,' he told himself. 'I suppose I was supposed to get down on my knees and coax her.'

It was fine to dwell on the surety that it was all done with. Mr Durant had somewhere picked up a phrase that seemed ideally suited to the occasion. It was to him an admirably dashing expression. There was something stylish about it; it was the sort of thing you would expect to hear used by men who wore spats and swung canes without self-consciousness. He employed it now, with satisfaction.

'Well, that's that,' he said to himself. He was not sure that he didn't say it aloud.

The car slowed, and the girl in the rough coat came down toward the door. She was jolted against Mr Durant – he would have sworn she did it purposely – uttered a word of laughing apology, gave him what he interpreted as an inviting glance. He half rose to follow her, then sank back again. After all, it was a wet night, and his corner was five blocks farther on. Again there came over him the cozy assurance that there would always be others.

In high humor, he left the car at his street, and walked in the direction of his house. It was a mean night, but the insinuating cold and the black rain only made more graphic his picture of the warm, bright house, the great dish of steaming fish chowder, the well-behaved children and wife that awaited him. He walked rather slowly to make them seem all the better for the wait, humming a little on his way down the neat sidewalk, past the solid, reputably shabby houses.

Two girls ran past him, holding their hands over their heads to protect their hats from the wet. He enjoyed the click of their heels on the pavement, their little bursts of breathless laughter, their arms upraised in a position that brought out all the neat lines of their bodies. He knew who they were – they lived three doors down from him, in the house with the lamp-post in front of it. He had often lingeringly noticed their fresh prettiness. He hurried, so that he might see them run up the steps, their narrow skirts sliding up over their legs. His mind went back to the girl with the run in her stocking, and amusing thoughts filled him as he entered his own house.

His children rushed, clamoring, to meet him, as he unlocked the door. There was something exciting going on, for Junior and Charlotte were usually too careful-mannered to cause people discomfort by rushing and babbling. They were nice, sensible children, good at their lessons, and punctilious about brushing their teeth, speaking the truth, and avoiding playmates who used bad words. Junior would be the very picture of his father, when they got the bands off his teeth, and little Charlotte strongly resembled her mother. Friends often commented on what a nice arrangement it was.

Mr Durant smiled good-naturedly through their racket, carefully hanging up his coat and hat. There was even pleasure for him in the arrangement of his apparel on the cool, shiny knob of the hatrack. Everything was pleasant, tonight. Even the children's noise couldn't irritate him.

Eventually he discovered the cause of the commotion. It was a little stray dog that had come to the back door. They were out in the kitchen helping Freda, and Charlotte thought she heard something scratching, and Freda said nonsense, but Charlotte went to the door, anyway, and there was this little dog, trying to get in out of the wet. Mother helped them give it a bath, and Freda fed it, and now it was in the living-room. Oh, Father, couldn't they keep it, please, couldn't they, couldn't they, please, Father, couldn't they? It didn't have any collar on it – so you see it didn't belong to anybody. Mother said all right, if he said so, and Freda liked it fine.

Mr Durant still smiled his gentle smile. 'We'll see,' he said.

The children looked disappointed, but not despondent. They would have liked more enthusiasm, but 'we'll see,' they knew by experience, meant a leaning in the right direction.

Mr Durant proceeded to the living-room, to inspect the visitor. It was not a beauty. All too obviously, it was the living souvenir of a mother who had never been able to say no. It was a rather stocky little beast with shaggy white hair and occasional, rakishly placed patches of black. There was a suggestion of Sealyham terrier about it, but that was almost blotted out by hosts of reminiscences of other breeds. It looked, on the whole, like a composite photograph of Popular Dogs. But you could tell at a glance that it had a way with it. Scepters have been tossed aside for that.

It lay, now, by the fire, waving its tragically long tail wistfully, its eyes pleading with Mr Durant to give it a fair trial. The children had told it to lie down there, and so it did not move. That was something it could do toward repaying them.

Mr Durant warmed to it. He did not dislike dogs, and

73

he somewhat fancied the picture of himself as a soft-hearted fellow who extended shelter to friendless animals. He bent, and held out a hand to it.

'Well, sir,' he said, genially. 'Come here, good fellow.'

The dog ran to him, wriggling ecstatically. It covered his cold hand with joyous, though respectful kisses, then laid its warm, heavy head on his palm. 'You are beyond a doubt the greatest man in America,' it told him with its eyes.

Mr Durant enjoyed appreciation and gratitude. He patted the dog graciously.

'Well, sir, how'd you like to board with us?' he said. 'I guess you can plan to settle down.' Charlotte squeezed Junior's arm wildly. Neither of them, though, thought it best to crowd their good fortune by making any immediate comment on it.

Mrs Durant entered from the kitchen, flushed with her final attentions to the chowder. There was a worried line between her eyes. Part of the worry was due to the dinner, and part to the disturbing entrance of the little dog into the family life. Anything not previously included in her day's schedule threw Mrs Durant into a state resembling that of one convalescing from shellshock. Her hands jerked nervously, beginning gestures that they never finished.

Relief smoothed her face when she saw her husband patting the dog. The children, always at ease with her, broke their silence and jumped about her, shrieking that Father said it might stay.

'There, now – didn't I tell you what a dear, good father you had?' she said in the tone parents employ when they have happened to guess right. 'That's fine, Father. With that big yard and all, I think we'll make out all right. She really seems to be an awfully good little—'

Mr Durant's hand stopped sharply in its patting motions, as if the dog's neck had become red-hot to his touch. He rose, and looked at his wife as at a stranger who had suddenly begun to behave wildly.

'She?' he said. He maintained the look and repeated the word. 'She?'

Mrs Durant's hands jerked.

'Well –' she began, as if about to plunge into a recital of extenuating circumstances. 'Well – yes,' she concluded.

The children and the dog looked nervously at Mr Durant, feeling something was gone wrong. Charlotte whimpered wordlessly.

'Quiet!' said her father, turning suddenly upon her. 'I said it could stay, didn't I? Did you ever know Father to break a promise?'

Charlotte politely murmured, 'No, Father,' but conviction was not hers. She was a philosophical child, though, and she decided to leave the whole issue to God, occasionally jogging Him up a bit with prayer.

Mr Durant frowned at his wife, and jerked his head backward. This indicated that he wished to have a few words with her, for adults only, in the privacy of the little room across the hall, known as 'Father's den.'

He had directed the decoration of his den, had seen that it had been made a truly masculine room. Red paper covered its walls, up to the wooden rack on which were displayed ornamental steins, of domestic manufacture. Empty pipe-racks – Mr Durant smoked cigars – were nailed against the red paper at frequent intervals. On one wall was an indifferent reproduction of a drawing of a young woman with wings like a vampire bat, and on another, a watercolored photograph of 'September Morn,' the tints running a bit beyond the edges of the figure as if the artist's emotions had rendered his hand unsteady. Over the table was carefully flung a tanned and fringed hide with the profile of an unknown Indian maiden painted on it, and the rocking-chair held a leather pillow bearing the picture, done by pyrography, of a girl in a fencing costume which set off her distressingly dated figure.

Mr Durant's books were lined up behind the glass of the bookcase. They were all tall, thick books, brightly bound, and they justified his pride in their showing. They were mostly accounts of favorites of the French court, with a few volumes on odd personal habits of various monarchs, and the adventures of former Russian monks. Mrs Durant, who never had time to get around to reading, regarded them with awe, and thought of her husband as one of the country's leading bibliophiles. There were books, too, in the living-room, but those she had inherited or been given. She had arranged a few on the living-room table; they looked as if they had been placed there by the Gideons.

Mr Durant thought of himself as an indefatigable collector and an insatiable reader. But he was always disappointed in his books, after he had sent for them. They were never so good as the advertisements had led him to believe.

Into his den Mr Durant preceded his wife, and faced her, still frowning. His calm was not shattered, but it was punctured. Something annoying always had to go and come up. Wouldn't you know?

'Now you know perfectly well, Fan, we can't have that dog around,' he told her. He used the low voice reserved for underwear and bathroom articles and kindred shady topics. There was all the kindness in his tones that one has for a backward child, but a Gibraltar-like firmness was behind it. 'You must be crazy to even think we could for a minute. Why, I wouldn't give a she-dog houseroom, not for any amount of money. It's disgusting, that's what it is.'

'Well, but, Father –' began Mrs Durant, her hands again going off into their convulsions.

'Disgusting,' he repeated. 'You have a female around, and you know what happens. All the males in the neighborhood will be running after her. First thing you know, she'd be having puppies – and the way they look after they've had them, and all! That would be nice for the children to see, wouldn't it? I should think you'd think of the children, Fan. No, sir, there'll be nothing like that around here, not while I know it. Disgusting!'

'But the children,' she said. 'They'll be just simply—'

'Now you just leave all that to me,' he reassured her. 'I told them the dog could stay, and I've never broken a promise yet, have I? Here's what I'll do – I'll wait till they're asleep, and then I'll just take this little dog and put it out. Then, in the morning, you can tell them it ran away during the night, see?'

She nodded. Her husband patted her shoulder, in its crapy-smelling black silk. His peace with the world was once more intact, restored by this simple solution of the little difficulty. Again his mind wrapped itself in the knowledge that everything was all fixed, all ready for a nice, fresh start. His arm was still about his wife's shoulder as they went on in to dinner.

Just a Little One

I like this place, Fred. This is a nice place. How did you ever find it? I think you're perfectly marvelous, discovering a speakeasy in the year 1928. And they let you right in, without asking you a single question. I bet you could get into the subway without using anybody's name. Couldn't you, Fred?

Oh, I like this place better and better, now that my eyes are getting accustomed to it. You mustn't let them tell you this lighting system is original with them, Fred; they got the idea from the Mammoth Cave. This is you sitting next to me, isn't it? Oh, you can't fool me. I'd know that knee anywhere.

You know what I like about this place? It's got atmosphere. That's what it's got. If you would ask the waiter to bring a fairly sharp knife, I could cut off a nice little block of the atmosphere, to take home with me. It would be interesting to have for my memory book. I'm going to start keeping a memory book tomorrow. Don't let me forget.

Why, I don't know, Fred – what are you going to have? Then I guess I'll have a highball, too; please, just a little one. Is it really real Scotch? Well, that will be a new experience for me. You ought to see the Scotch I've got home in my cupboard; at least it was in the cupboard this morning – it's probably eaten its way out by now. I got it for my birthday. Well, it was something. The birthday before, all I got was a year older.

This is a nice highball, isn't it? Well, well, well, to think of me having real Scotch; I'm out of the bush leagues at last. Are you going to have another one? Well, I shouldn't like to see you drinking all by yourself, Fred. Solitary drinking is what causes half the crime in the country. That's what's responsible for the failure of prohibition. But please, Fred, tell him to make mine just a little one. Make it awfully weak; just cambric Scotch.

It will be nice to see the effect of veritable whisky upon one who has been accustomed only to the simpler forms of entertainment. You'll like that, Fred. You'll stay by me if anything happens, won't you? I don't think there will be anything spectacular, but I want to ask you one thing, just in case. Don't let me take any horses home with me. It doesn't matter so much about stray dogs and kittens, but elevator boys get awfully stuffy when you try to bring in a horse. You might just as well know that about me now, Fred. You can always tell that the crash is coming when I start getting tender about Our Dumb Friends. Three highballs, and I think I'm St Francis of Assisi.

But I don't believe anything is going to happen to me on these. That's because they're made of real stuff. That's what the difference is. This just makes you feel fine. Oh, I feel swell, Fred. You do too, don't you? I knew you did, because you look better. I love that tie you have on. Oh, did Edith give it to you? Ah, wasn't that nice of her? You know, Fred, most people are really awfully nice. There are darn few that aren't pretty fine at heart. You've got a beautiful heart, Fred. You'd be the first person I'd go to if I were in trouble. I guess you are just about the best friend I've got in the world. But I worry about you, Fred. I do so, too. I don't think you take enough care of yourself. You ought to take care of yourself for your friends' sake. You oughtn't to drink all this terrible stuff that's around; you owe it to your friends to be careful. You don't mind my talking to you like this, do you? You see, dear, it's because I'm your friend that I hate to see you not taking care of yourself. It hurts me to see you batting around the way you've been doing. You ought to stick to this place, where they have real Scotch that can't do you any harm. Oh, darling, do you really think I ought to? Well, you tell him just a little bit of a one. Tell him, sweet.

Do you come here often, Fred? I shouldn't worry about you so much if I knew you were in a safe place like this. Oh, is this where you were Thursday night? I see. Why, no, it didn't make a bit of difference, only you told me to call you up, and like a fool I broke a date I had, just because I thought I was going to see you. I just sort of naturally thought so, when you said to call you up. Oh, good Lord, don't make all that fuss about it. It really didn't make the slightest difference. It just didn't seem a very friendly way to behave, that's all. I don't know – I'd been believing we were such good friends. I'm an awful idiot about people, Fred. There aren't many who are really your friend at heart. Practically anybody would play you dirt for a nickel. Oh, yes, they would.

Was Edith here with you, Thursday night? This place must be very becoming to her. Next to being in a coal mine, I can't think of anywhere she could go that the light would be more flattering to that pan of hers. Do you really know a lot of people that say she's good-looking? You must have a wide acquaintance among the astigmatic, haven't you, Freddie, dear? Why, I'm not being any way at all – it's simply one of those things, either you can see it or you can't. Now to me, Edith looks like something that would eat her young. Dresses well? *Edith* dresses well? Are you trying to kid me, Fred, at my age? You mean you mean it? Oh, my God. You mean those clothes of hers are *intentional*? My heavens, I always thought she was on her way out of a burning building.

Well, we live and learn. Edith dresses well! Edith's got good taste! Yes, she's got sweet taste in neckties. I don't suppose I ought to say it about such a dear friend of yours, Fred, but she is the lousiest necktie-picker-out I ever saw. I never saw anything could touch that thing you have around your neck. All right, suppose I did say I liked it. I just said that because I felt sorry for you. I'd feel sorry for anybody with a thing like that on. I just wanted to try to make you feel good, because I thought you were my friend. My friend! I haven't got a friend in the world. Do you know that, Fred? Not one single friend in this world.

All right, what do you care if I'm crying, I can cry if I want to, can't I? I guess you'd cry, too, if you didn't have a friend in the world. Is my face very bad? I suppose that damned mascara has run all over it. I've got to give up using mascara, Fred; life's too sad. Isn't life terrible? Oh, my God, isn't life awful? Ah, don't cry, Fred. Please don't. Don't you care, baby. Life's terrible, but don't you care. You've got friends. I'm the one that hasn't got any friends. I am so. No, it's me. I'm the one.

I don't think another drink would make me feel any better. I don't know whether I want to feel any better. What's the sense of feeling good, when life's so terrible? Oh, all right, then. But please tell him just a little one, if it isn't too much trouble. I don't want to stay here much longer. I don't like this place. It's all dark and stuffy. It's the kind of place Edith would be crazy about – that's all I can say about this place. I know I oughtn't to talk about your best friend, Fred, but that's a terrible woman. That woman is the louse of this world. It makes me feel just awful that you trust that woman, Fred. I hate to see anybody play you dirt. I'd hate to see you get hurt. That's what makes me feel so terrible. That's why I'm getting mascara all over my face. No, please don't, Fred. You mustn't hold my hand. It wouldn't be fair to Edith. We've got to play fair with the big louse. After all, she's your best friend, isn't she?

Honestly? Do you honestly mean it, Fred? Yes, but how could I help thinking so, when you're with her all the time – when you bring her here every night in the week? Really, only Thursday? Oh, I know – I know how those things are. You simply can't help it, when you get stuck with a person that way. Lord, I'm glad you realize what an awful thing that woman is. I was worried about it, Fred. It's because I'm your friend. Why, of course I am, darling. You know I am. Oh, that's just silly, Freddie. You've got heaps of friends. Only you'll never find a better friend than I am. No, I know that. I know I'll never find a better friend than you are to me. Just give me back my hand a second, till I get this damned mascara out of my eye.

Yes, I think we ought to, honey. I think we ought to have a little drink, on account of our being friends. Just a little one, because it's real Scotch, and we're real friends. After all, friends are the greatest things in the world, aren't they, Fred? Gee, it makes you feel good to know you have a friend. I feel great, don't you, dear? And you look great, too. I'm proud to have you for a friend. Do you realize, Fred, what a rare thing a friend is, when you think of all the terrible people there are in this world? Animals are much better than people. God, I love animals. That's what I like about you, Fred. You're so fond of animals.

Look, I'll tell you what let's do, after we've had just a little highball. Let's go out and pick up a lot of stray dogs.

I never had enough dogs in my life, did you? We ought to have more dogs. And maybe there'd be some cats around, if we looked. And a horse, I've never had one single horse, Fred. Isn't that rotten? Not one single horse. Ah, I'd like a nice old cab-horse, Fred. Wouldn't you? I'd like to take care of it and comb its hair and everything. Ah, don't be stuffy about it, Fred, please don't. I need a horse, honestly I do. Wouldn't you like one? It would be so sweet and kind. Let's have a drink and then let's you and I go out and get a horsie, Freddie – just a little one, darling, just a little one.

Little Curtis

Mrs Matson paused in the vestibule of G. Fosdick's Sons' Department Store. She transferred a small parcel from her right hand to the crook of her left arm, gripped her shopping-bag firmly by its German-silver frame, opened it with a capable click, and drew from its orderly interior a little black-bound book and a neatly sharpened pencil.

Shoppers passing in and out jostled her as she stood there, but they neither shared in Mrs Matson's attention nor hurried her movements. She made no answer to the 'Oh, I *beg* your pardons' that bubbled from the lips of the more tender-hearted among them. Calm, sure, gloriously aloof, Mrs Matson stood, opened her book, poised her pencil, and wrote in delicate, prettily slanting characters: '4 crepe-paper candy-baskets, $.28.'

The dollar-sign was gratifyingly decorative, the decimal point clear and deep, the 2 daintily curled, the 8 admirably balanced. Mrs Matson looked approvingly at her handiwork. Still unhurried, she closed the book, replaced it and the pencil in the bag, tested the snap to see that it was indisputably shut, and took the parcel once more in her right hand. Then, with a comfortable air of duty well done, she passed impressively, and with a strong push, from G. Fosdick's Sons' Department Store by means of a portal which bore a placard with the request, 'Please Use Other Door.'

Slowly Mrs Matson made her way down Maple Street. The morning sunshine that flooded the town's main thoroughfare caused her neither to squint nor to lower her face. She held her head high, looking about her as one who says, 'Our good people, we are pleased with you.'

She stopped occasionally by a shop-window, to inspect thoroughly the premature autumn costumes there displayed. But her heart was unfluttered by the envy which attacked the lesser women around her. Though her long black coat, of that vintage when coats were puffed of sleeve and cut sharply in at the waist, was stained and shiny, and her hat had the general air of indecision and lack of spirit that comes with age, and her elderly black gloves were worn in patches of rough gray, Mrs Matson had no yearnings for the fresh, trim costumes set temptingly before her. Snug in her was the thought of the rows of recent garments, each one in its flowered cretonne casing, occupying the varnished hangers along the poles of her bedroom closet.

She had her unalterable ideas about such people as gave or threw away garments that might still be worn, for warmth and modesty, if not for style. She found it distinctly lower-class to wear one's new clothes 'for every day'; there was an unpleasant suggestion of extravagance and riotous living in the practice. The working classes, who, as Mrs Matson often explained to her friends, went and bought themselves electric ice-boxes and radios the minute they got a little money, did such things.

No morbid thought of her possible sudden demise before the clothes in her closet could be worn or enjoyed irked her. Life's uncertainty was not for those of her position. Mrs Matsons pass away between seventy and eighty; sometimes later, never before.

A blind colored woman, a tray of pencils hung about her neck, with a cane tapping the pavement before her, came down the street. Mrs Matson swerved sharply to the curb to avoid her, wasting a withering glance upon her. It was Mrs Matson's immediate opinion that the woman could see as well as *she* could. She never bought of the poor on the streets, and was angry if she saw others do so. She frequently remarked that these beggars all had big bank-accounts.

She crossed to the car-tracks to await the trolley that would bear her home, her calm upset by her sight of the woman. 'Probably owns an apartment-house,' she told herself, and shot an angry glance after the blind woman.

However, her poise was restored by the act of tendering her fare to the courteous conductor. Mrs Matson rather enjoyed small and legitimate disbursements to those who were appropriately grateful. She gave him her nickel with the manner of one presenting a park to a city, and swept into the car to a desirable seat.

Settled, with the parcel securely wedged between her hip and the window, against loss or robbery, Mrs Matson again produced the book and pencil. 'Car-fare, $.05,' she wrote. Again the exquisite handwriting, the neat figures, gave her a flow of satisfaction.

Mrs Matson, regally without acknowledgment, accepted the conductor's aid in alighting from the car at her corner. She trod the sun-splashed pavement, bowing now and again to neighbors knitting on their porches or bending solicitously over their iris-beds. Slow, stately bows she gave, unaccompanied by smile or word of greeting. After all, she was Mrs Albert Matson; she had been Miss Laura Whitmore, of the Drop Forge and Tool Works Whitmores. One does not lose sight of such things.

She always enjoyed the first view of her house as she walked toward it. It amplified in her her sense of security and permanence. There it stood, in its tidy, treeless lawns, square and solid and serviceable. You thought of steel-engravings and rows of Scott's novels behind glass, and Sunday dinner in the middle of the day, when you looked at it. You knew immediately that within it no one ever banged a door, no one clattered up- and down-stairs, no one spilled crumbs or dropped ashes or left the light burning in the bathroom.

Expectancy pervaded Mrs Matson as she approached her home. She spoke of it always as her home. 'You must come to see me in my home some time,' she graciously commanded new acquaintances. There was a large, institutional sound to it that you didn't get in the word 'house.'

She liked to think of its cool, high-ceilinged rooms, of its busy maids, of little Curtis waiting to deliver her his respectful kiss. She had adopted him almost a year ago, when he was four. She had, she told her friends, never once regretted it.

In her absence her friends had been wont to comment sadly upon what a shame it was that the Albert Matsons had no child – and with all the Matson and Whitmore money, too. Neither of them, the friends pointed out, could live forever; it would all have to go to the Henry Matson's children. And they were but quoting Mrs Albert Matson's own words when they observed that those children would be just the kind that would run right through it.

Mr and Mrs Matson held a joint view of the devastation that would result if their nephews and nieces were ever turned loose among the Matson and Whitmore money. As is frequent in such instances, their worry led them to pay the other Matson family the compliment of the credit for schemes and desires that had never edged into their thoughts.

The Albert Matsons saw their relatives as waiting, with a sort of stalking patience, for the prayed-for moment of their death. For years they conjured up ever more lurid pictures of the Matson children going through their money like Sherman to the sea; for years they carried about with them the notion that their demise was being eagerly awaited, was being made, indeed, the starting-point of bacchanalian plans.

The Albert Matsons were as one in everything, as in this. Their thoughts, their manners, their opinions, their very locutions were phenomena of similarity. People even pointed out that Mr and Mrs Matson looked alike. It was regarded as the world's misfortune that so obviously Heaven-made a match was without offspring. And of course – you always had to come back to it, it bulked so before you – there was all that Matson and Whitmore money.

No one, though, ever directly condoled with Mrs Matson upon her childlessness. In her presence one didn't speak of things like having children. She accepted the fact of babies when they were shown to her; she fastidiously disregarded their mode of arrival.

She had told none of her friends of her decision to adopt a little boy. No one knew about it until the papers were signed and he was established in the Matson house. Mrs Matson had got him, she explained, 'at the best place in New York.' No one was surprised at that. Mrs Matson always went to the best places when she shopped in New York. You thought of her selecting a child as she selected all her other belongings: a good one, one that would last.

She stopped abruptly now, as she came to her gate, a

sudden frown creasing her brow. Two little boys, too absorbed to hear her steps, were playing in the hot sun by the hedge – two little boys much alike in age, size, and attire, compact, pink-and-white, good little boys, their cheeks flushed with interest, the backs of their necks warm and damp. They played an interminable, mysterious game with pebbles and twigs and a small tin trolley-car.

Mrs Matson entered the yard.

'Curtis!' she said.

Both little boys looked up, startled. One of them rose and hung his head before her frown.

'And who,' said Mrs Matson deeply, 'who told Georgie he could come here?'

No answer. Georgie, still squatting on his heels, looked inquiringly from her to Curtis. He was interested and unalarmed.

'Was it you, Curtis?' asked Mrs Matson.

Curtis nodded. You could scarcely tell that he did, his head hung so low.

'Yes, mother dear!' said Mrs Matson.

'Yes, mother dear,' whispered Curtis.

'And how many times,' Mrs Matson inquired, 'have I told you that you were not to play with Georgie? How many times, Curtis?'

Curtis murmured vaguely. He wished that Georgie would please go.

'You don't know?' said Mrs Matson incredulously. 'You don't know? After all mother does for you, you don't

know how many times she has told you not to play with
Georgie? Don't you remember what mother told you she'd
have to do if you ever played with Georgie again?'

A pause. Then the nod.

'Yes, mother dear!' said Mrs Matson.

'Yes, mother dear,' said Curtis.

'Well!' Mrs Matson said. She turned to the enthralled
Georgie. 'You'll have to go home now, Georgie – go right
straight home. And you're not to come here any more,
do you understand me? Curtis is not allowed to play with
you – not ever.'

Georgie rose.

' 'By,' he said philosophically, and walked away, his
farewell unanswered.

Mrs Matson gazed upon Curtis. Grief disarranged her
features.

'Playing!' she said, her voice broken with emotion.
'Playing with a furnaceman's child! After all mother does
for you!'

She took him by a limp arm and led him, unresisting,
along the walk to the house; led him past the maid that
opened the door, up the stairs to his little blue bedroom.
She put him in it and closed the door.

Then she went to her own room, placed her package
carefully on the table, removed her gloves, and laid them,
with her bag, in an orderly drawer. She entered her closet,
hung up her coat, then stooped for one of the felt slippers
that were set scrupulously, in the first dancing position,

on the floor beneath her nightgown. It was a lavender slipper, with scallops and a staid rosette; it had a light, flexible leather sole, across which was stamped its name, 'Kumfy-Toes.'

Mrs Matson grasped it firmly by the heel and flicked it back and forth. Carrying it, she went to the little boy's room. She began to speak as she turned the door-knob.

'And before mother had time to take her hat off, too,' she said. The door closed behind her.

She came out again presently. A scale of shrieks followed her.

'That will do!' she announced, looking back from the door. The shrieks faded obediently to sobs. 'That's quite enough of that, thank you. Mother's had just about plenty for one morning. And today, too, with the ladies coming this afternoon, and all mother has to attend to! Oh, I'd be ashamed, Curtis, if I were you – that's what I'd be.'

She closed the door, and retired, to remove her hat.

The ladies came in mid-afternoon. There were three of them. Mrs Kerley, gray and brittle and painstaking, always thoughtful about sending birthday-cards and carrying glass jars of soup to the sick. Mrs Swan, her visiting sister-in-law, younger, and given to daisied hats and crocheted lace collars, with her transient's air of bright, determined interest in her hostess's acquaintaces and activities. And Mrs Cook. Only she did not count very much. She was extremely deaf, and so pretty well out of things.

She had visited innumerable specialists, spent uncounted money, endured agonizing treatments, in her endeavors to be able to hear what went on about her and to have a part in it. They had finally fitted her out with a long, coiling, corrugated speaking-tube, rather like a larger intestine. One end of this she placed in her better ear, and the other she extended to those who would hold speech with her. But the shining black mouthpiece seemed to embarrass people and intimidate them; they could think of nothing better to call into it than 'Getting colder out,' or 'You keeping pretty well?' To hear such remarks as these she had gone through years of suffering.

Mrs Matson, in her last spring's blue taffeta, assigned her guests to seats about the living-room. It was an afternoon set apart for fancy-work and conversation. Later there would be tea, and two triangular sandwiches apiece made from the chopped remnants of last night's chicken, and a cake which was a high favorite with Mrs Matson, for its formula required but one egg. She had gone, in person, to the kitchen to supervise its making. She was not entirely convinced that her cook was wasteful of materials, but she felt that the woman would bear watching.

The crepe-paper baskets, fairly well filled with disks of peppermint creams, were to enliven the corners of the tea-table. Mrs Matson trusted her guests not to regard them as favors and take them home.

The conversation dealt, and favorably, with the weather.

Mrs Kerley and Mrs Swan vied with each other in paying compliments to the day.

'So clear,' said Mrs Kerley.

'Not a cloud in the sky,' augmented Mrs Swan. 'Not a one.'

'The air was just lovely this morning,' reported Mrs Kerley. 'I said to myself, "Well, this is a beautiful day if there ever *was* one."'

'There's something so balmy about it,' said Mrs Swan.

Mrs Cook spoke suddenly and overloudly, in the untrustworthy voice of the deaf.

'Phew, this is a scorcher!' she said. 'Something terrible out.'

The conversation went immediately to literature. It developed that Mrs Kerley had been reading a lovely book. Its name and that of its author escaped her at the moment, but her enjoyment of it was so keen that she had lingered over it till 'way past ten o'clock the night before. Particularly did she commend its descriptions of some of those Italian places; they were, she affirmed, just like a picture. The book had been drawn to her attention by the young woman at the Little Booke Nooke. It was, on her authority, one of the new ones.

Mrs Matson frowned at her embroidery. Words flowed readily from her lips. She seemed to have spoken on the subject before.

'I haven't any use for all these new books,' she said. 'I wouldn't give them house-room. I don't see why a person wants to sit down and write any such stuff. I often think, I don't believe they know what they're writing about themselves half the time. I don't know who they think wants to read those kind of things. I'm sure *I* don't.'

She paused to let her statements sink deep.

'Mr Matson,' she continued – she always spoke of her husband thus; it conveyed an aristocratic sense of aloofness, did away with any suggestion of carnal intimacy between them – 'Mr Matson isn't any hand for these new books, either. He always says, if he could find another book like *David Harum*, he'd read it in a minute. I wish,' she added longingly, 'I had a dollar for every time I've heard him say that.'

Mrs Kerley smiled. Mrs Swan threw a rippling little laugh into the pause.

'Well, it's true, you know, it really is true,' Mrs Kerley told Mrs Swan.

'Oh, it is,' Mrs Swan hastened to reassure her.

'I don't know what we're coming to, *I'm* sure,' announced Mrs Matson.

She sewed, her thread twanging through the tight-stretched circle of linen in her embroidery-hoop.

The stoppage of conversation weighed upon Mrs Swan. She lifted her head and looked out the window.

'My, what a lovely lawn you have!' she said. 'I couldn't help noticing it, first thing. We've been living in New York, you know.'

'I often say I don't see what people want to shut

themselves up in a place like that for,' Mrs Matson said. 'You know, you exist, in New York – we live, out here.'

Mrs Swan laughed a bit nervously. Mrs Kerley nodded. 'That's right,' she said. 'That's pretty good.'

Mrs Matson herself thought it worthy of repetition. She picked up Mrs Cook's speaking-tube.

'I was just saying to Mrs Swan,' she cried, and called her epigram into the mouthpiece.

'Live where?' asked Mrs Cook.

Mrs Matson smiled at her patiently. 'New York. You know, that's where I got my little adopted boy.'

'Oh, yes,' said Mrs Swan. 'Carrie told me. Now, wasn't that lovely of you!'

Mrs Matson shrugged. 'Yes,' she said, 'I went right to the best place for him. Miss Codman's nursery – it's absolutely reliable. You can get awfully nice children there. There's quite a long waiting-list, they tell me.'

'Goodness, just think how it must seem to him to be up here,' said Mrs Swan, 'with this big house, and that lovely, smooth lawn, and everything.'

Mrs Matson laughed slightly. 'Oh – well,' she said.

'I hope he appreciates it,' remarked Mrs Swan.

'I think he will,' Mrs Matson said capably. 'Of course,' she conceded, 'he's pretty young right now.'

'So lovely,' murmured Mrs Swan. 'So sweet to get them young like this and have them grow up.'

'Yes, I think that's the nicest way,' agreed Mrs Matson. 'And, you know, I really enjoy training him. Naturally, now that we have him here with us, we want him to act like a little gentleman.'

'Just think of it,' cried Mrs Swan, 'a child like that having all this! And will you have him go to school later on?'

'Oh, yes,' Mrs Matson replied. 'Yes, we want him to be educated. You take a child going to some nice little school near here, say, where he'll meet only the best children, and he'll make friends that it will be a pretty good thing for him to know some day.'

Mrs Swan waxed arch. 'I suppose you've got it all settled what he's going to be when he grows up,' she said.

'Why, certainly,' said Mrs Matson. 'He's to go right straight into Mr Matson's business. My husband,' she informed Mrs Swan, 'is the Matson Adding Machines.'

'Oh-h-h,' said Mrs Swan on a descending scale.

'I think Curtis will do very well in school,' prophesied Mrs Matson. 'He's not at all stupid – picks up everything. Mr Matson is anxious to have him brought up to be a good, sensible business man – he says that's what this country needs, you know. So I've been trying to teach him the value of money. I've bought him a little bank. I don't think you can begin too early. Because probably some day Curtis is going to have – well—'

Mrs Matson drifted into light, anecdotal mood.

'Oh, it's funny the way children are,' she remarked. 'The other day Mrs Newman brought her little Amy down to play with Curtis, and when I went up to look at them, there he was, trying to give her his brand-new flannel rabbit. So I just took him into my room, and I sat him down, and I said to him, "Now, Curtis," I said, "you must realize that mother had to pay almost two dollars for that rabbit – nearly two hundred pennies," I said. "It's very nice to be generous, but you must learn that it isn't a good idea to give things away to people. Now you go in to Amy," I said, "and you tell her you're sorry, but she'll have to give that rabbit right back to you."'

'And did he do it?' asked Mrs Swan.

'Why, I told him to,' Mrs Matson said.

'Isn't it splendid?' Mrs Swan asked of the company at large. 'Really, when you think of it. A child like that, just suddenly having everything all at once. And probably coming of poor people, too. Are his parents – living?'

'Oh, no, no,' Mrs Matson said briskly. 'I couldn't be bothered with anything like that. Of course, I found out all about them. They were really quite nice, clean people – the father was a college man. Curtis really comes of a very nice family, for an orphan.'

'Do you think you'll ever tell him that you aren't – that he isn't – tell him about it?' inquired Mrs Kerley.

'Dear me, yes, just as soon as he's a little older,' Mrs Matson answered. 'I think it's so much nicer for him to know. He'll appreciate everything so much more.'

'Does the little thing remember his father and mother at all?' Mrs Swan asked.

'*I* really don't know if he does or not,' said Mrs Matson.

'Tea,' announced the maid, appearing abruptly at the door.

'Tea is served, Mrs Matson,' said Mrs Matson, her voice lifted.

'Tea is served, Mrs Matson,' echoed the maid.

'I don't know what I'm going to do with her,' Mrs Matson told her guests when the girl had disappeared. 'Here last night she had company in the kitchen till nearly eleven o'clock at night. The trouble with me is I'm too good to servants. The only way to do is to treat them like cattle.'

'They don't appreciate anything else,' said Mrs Kerley.

Mrs Matson placed her embroidery in her sweet-grass workbasket, and rose.

'Well, shall we go have a cup of tea?' she said.

'Why, how lovely!' cried Mrs Swan.

Mrs Cook, who had been knitting doggedly, was informed, via the speaking-tube, of the readiness of tea. She dropped her work instantly, and led the way to the dining-room.

The talk, at the tea-table, was of stitches and patterns. Praise, benignly accepted by Mrs Matson, was spread by Mrs Swan and Mrs Kerley upon the sandwiches, the cake, the baskets, the table-linen, the china, and the design of the silver.

A watch was glanced at, and there arose cries of surprise at the afternoon's flight. There was an assembling of workbags, a fluttering exodus to the hall to put on hats. Mrs Matson watched her guests.

'Well, it's been just too lovely,' Mrs Swan declared, clasping her hand. 'I can't *tell* you how much I've enjoyed it, hearing about the dear little boy, and all. I *hope* you're going to let me see him some time.'

'Why, you can see him now, if you'd like,' said Mrs Matson. She went to the foot of the stairs and sang, '*Cur*-tis, *Cur*-tis.'

Curtis appeared in the hall above, clean in the gray percale sailor-suit that had been selected in the thrifty expectation of his 'growing into it.' He looked down at them, caught sight of Mrs Cook's speaking-tube, and watched it intently, his eyes wide open.

'Come down and see the ladies, Curtis,' commanded Mrs Matson.

Curtis came down, his warm hand squeaking along the banister. He placed his right foot upon a step, brought his left foot carefully down to it, then started his right one off again. Eventually he reached them.

'Can't you say how-do-you-do to the ladies?' asked Mrs Matson.

He gave each guest, in turn, a small, flaccid hand.

Mrs Swan squatted suddenly before him, so that her face was level with his.

'My, what a nice boy!' she cried. 'I just love little boys like you, do you know it? Ooh, I could just eat you up! I could!'

She squeezed his arms. Curtis, in alarm, drew his head back from her face.

'And what's *your* name?' she asked him. 'Let's see if you can tell me what your name is. I just *bet* you can't!'

He looked at her.

'Can't you tell the lady your name, Curtis?' demanded Mrs Matson.

'Curtis,' he told the lady.

'Why, what a *pretty* name!' she cried. She looked up at Mrs Matson. 'Was that his real name?' she asked.

'No,' Mrs Matson said, 'they had him called something else. But I named him as soon as I got him. My mother was a Curtis.'

Thus might one say, 'My name was Guelph before I married.'

Mrs Cook spoke sharply. 'Lucky!' she said. 'Pretty lucky, that young one!'

'Well, I should say so,' echoed Mrs Swan. 'Aren't you a pretty lucky little boy? Aren't you, aren't you, aren't you?' She rubbed her nose against his.

'Yes, Mrs Swan.' Mrs Matson pronounced and frowned at Curtis.

He murmured something.

'Ooh – *you*!' said Mrs Swan. She rose from her squatting posture. 'I'd like to *steal* you, in your little sailor-suit, and all!'

'Mother bought that suit for you, didn't she?' asked Mrs Matson of Curtis. 'Mother bought him all his nice things.'

'Oh, he calls you mother? Now, isn't that sweet!' cried Mrs Swan.

'Yes, I think it's nice,' said Mrs Matson.

There was a brisk, sure step on the porch; a key turned in the lock. Mr Matson was among them.

'Well,' said Mrs Matson upon seeing her mate. It was her invariable evening greeting to him.

'Ah,' said Mr Matson. It was his to her.

Mrs Kerley cooed. Mrs Swan blinked vivaciously. Mrs Cook applied her speaking-tube to her ear in the anticipation of hearing something good.

'I don't think you've met Mrs Swan, Albert,' remarked Mrs Matson. He bowed.

'Oh, I've heard so much about Mr Matson,' cried Mrs Swan.

Again he bowed.

'We've been making friends with your dear little boy,' Mrs Swan said. She pinched Curtis's cheek. 'You sweetie, you!'

'Well, Curtis,' said Mr Matson, 'haven't you got a good-evening for me?'

Curtis gave his hand to his present father with a weak smile of politeness. He looked modestly down.

'That's more like it,' summarized Mr Matson. His parental duties accomplished, he turned to fulfill his social obligations. Boldly he caught up Mrs Cook's speaking-tube. Curtis watched.

'Getting cooler out,' roared Mr Matson. 'I thought it would.'

Mrs Cook nodded. 'That's good!' she shouted.

Mr Matson pressed forward to open the door for her. He was of generous proportions, and the hall was narrow. One of the buttons-of-leisure on his coat-sleeve caught in Mrs Cook's speaking-tube. It fell, with a startling crash, to the floor, and writhed about.

Curtis's control went. Peal upon peal of high, helpless laughter came from him. He laughed on, against Mrs Matson's cry of 'Curtis!,' against Mr Matson's frown. He doubled over with his hands on his little brown knees, and laughed mad laughter.

'Curtis!' bellowed Mr Matson. The laughter died. Curtis straightened himself, and one last little moan of enjoyment escaped him.

Mr Matson pointed with a magnificent gesture. 'Upstairs!' he boomed.

Curtis turned and climbed the stairs. He looked small beside the banister.

'Well, of all the –' said Mrs Matson. 'I never knew him to do a thing like that since he's been here. I never heard him do such a thing!'

'That young man,' pronounced Mr Matson, 'needs a good talking to.'

'He needs more than that,' his spouse said.

Mr Matson stooped with a faint creaking, retrieved

the speaking-tube, and presented it to Mrs Cook. 'Not at all,' he said in anticipation of the thanks which she left unspoken. He bowed.

'Pardon me,' he ordered, and mounted the stairs.

Mrs Matson moved to the door in the wake of her guests. She was bewildered and, it seemed, grieved.

'I never,' she affirmed, 'never knew that child to go on that way.'

'Oh, children,' Mrs Kerley assured her, 'they're funny sometimes – especially a little boy like that. You can't expect so much. My goodness, you'll fix all that! I always say I don't know any child that's getting any better bringing up than that young one – just as if he was your own.'

Peace returned to the breast of Mrs Matson. 'Oh – goodness!' she said. There was almost a coyness in her smile as she closed the door on the departing.

Lady with a Lamp

Well, Mona! Well, you poor sick thing, you! Ah, you look so little and white and *little*, you do, lying there in that great big bed. That's what you do – go and look so child-like and pitiful nobody'd have the heart to scold you. And I ought to scold you, Mona. Oh, yes, I should so, too. Never letting me know you were ill. Never a word to your oldest friend. Darling, you might have known I'd under-stand, no matter what you did. What do I mean? Well, what do you *mean* what do I mean, Mona? Of course, if you'd rather not talk about – Not even to your oldest friend. All I wanted to say was you might have known that I'm always for you, no matter what happens. I do admit, sometimes it's a little hard for me to understand how on earth you ever got into such – well. Goodness knows I don't want to nag you now, when you're so sick.

All right, Mona, then you're *not* sick. If that's what you want to say, even to me, why, all right, my dear. People who aren't sick have to stay in bed for nearly two weeks, I suppose; I suppose people who aren't sick look the way you do. Just your nerves? You were simply all tired out? I see. It's just your nerves. You were simply tired. Yes. Oh, Mona, Mona, why don't you feel you can trust me?

Well – if that's the way you want to be to me, that's the way you want to be. I won't say anything more about it. Only I do think you might have let me know that you had – well, that you were so *tired*, if that's what you want me to say. Why, I'd never have known a word about it if I hadn't run bang into Alice Patterson and she told me she'd called you up and that maid of yours said you had been sick in bed for ten days. Of course, I'd thought it rather funny I hadn't heard from you, but you know how you are – you simply let people go, and weeks can go by like, well, like *weeks*, and never a sign from you. Why, I could have been dead over and over again, for all you'd know. Twenty times over. Now, I'm not going to scold you when you're sick, but frankly and honestly, Mona, I said to myself this time, 'Well, she'll have a good wait before I call her up. I've given in often enough, goodness knows. Now she can just call me first.' Frankly and honestly, that's what I said!

And then I saw Alice, and I did feel mean, I really did. And now to see you lying there – well, I feel like a complete *dog*. That's what you do to people even when you're in the wrong the way you always are, you wicked little thing, you! Ah, the poor dear! Feels just so awful, doesn't it?

Oh, don't keep trying to be brave, child. Not with me. Just give in – it helps so much. Just tell me all about it. You know I'll never say a word. Or at least you ought to know. When Alice told me that maid of yours said you

were all tired out and your nerves had gone bad, I naturally never said anything, but I thought to myself, 'Well,
maybe that's the only thing Mona could say was the matter. That's probably about the best excuse she could think
of.' And of course *I'll* never deny it – but perhaps it might
have been better to have said you had influenza or pto-
maine poisoning. After all, people don't stay in bed for
ten whole days just because they're nervous. All right,
Mona, then they *do*. Then they do. Yes, dear.

Ah, to think of you going through all this and crawling
off here all alone like a little wounded animal or something.
And with only that colored Edie to take care of you. Darling, oughtn't you have a trained nurse, I mean really
oughtn't you? There must be so many things that have to
be done for you. Why, Mona! Mona, please! Dear, you
don't have to get so excited. Very well, my dear, it's just as
you say – there isn't a single thing to be done. I was mistaken, that's all. I simply thought that after – Oh, now, you
don't have to do that. You never have to say you're sorry,
to *me*. I understand. As a matter of fact, I was glad to hear
you lose your temper. It's a good sign when sick people are
cross. It means they're on the way to getting better. Oh, I
know! You go right ahead and be cross all you want to.

Look, where shall I sit? I want to sit some place where
you won't have to turn around, so you can talk to me. You
stay right the way you're lying, and I'll – Because you
shouldn't move around, I'm sure. It must be terribly bad
for you. All right, dear, you can move around all you want

to. All right, I must be crazy. I'm crazy, then. We'll leave it like that. Only please, please don't excite yourself that way.

I'll just get this chair and put it over – oops, I'm sorry I joggled the bed – put it over here, where you can see me. There. But first I want to fix your pillows before I get settled. Well, they certainly are *not* all right, Mona. After the way you've been twisting them and pulling them, these last few minutes. Now look, honey, I'll help you raise yourself ve-ry, ve-ry slo-o-ow-ly. Oh. Of course you can sit up by yourself, dear. Of course you can. Nobody ever said you couldn't. Nobody ever thought of such a thing. There now, your pillows are all smooth and lovely, and you lie right down again, before you hurt yourself. Now, isn't that better? Well, I should think it was!

Just a minute, till I get my sewing. Oh, yes, I brought it along, so we'd be all cozy. Do you honestly, frankly and honestly, think it's pretty? I'm so glad. It's nothing but a tray-cloth, you know. But you simply can't have too many. They're a lot of fun to make, too, doing this edge – it goes so quickly. Oh, Mona dear, so often I think if you just had a home of your own, and could be all busy, making pretty little things like this for it, it would do so *much* for you. I worry so about you, living in a little furnished apartment, with nothing that belongs to you, no roots, no nothing. It's not right for a woman. It's all wrong for a woman like you. Oh, I wish you'd get over that Garry McVicker! If you could just meet some nice, sweet, considerate man, and get married to him, and have your own lovely place – and with your *taste*, Mona! – and maybe have a couple of children. You're so simply adorable with children. Why, Mona Morrison, are you crying? Oh, you've got a cold? You've got a cold, *too?* I thought you were crying, there for a second. Don't you want my handkerchief, lamb? Oh, you have yours. Wouldn't you have a pink chiffon handkerchief, you nut! Why on earth don't you use cleansing tissues, just lying there in bed with no one to see you? You little idiot, you! Extravagant little fool!

No, but really, I'm serious. I've said to Fred so often, 'Oh, if we could just get Mona married!' Honestly, you don't know the feeling it gives you, just to be all secure and safe with your own sweet home and your own blessed children, and your own nice husband coming back to you every night. That's a woman's *life*, Mona. What you've been doing is really horrible. Just drifting along, that's all. What's going to happen to you, dear, whatever is going to become of you? But no – you don't even think of it. You go, and go falling in love with that Garry. Well, my dear, you've got to give me credit – I said from the very first, 'He'll never marry her.' You know that. What? There was never any thought of marriage, with you and Garry? Oh, Mona, now listen! Every woman on earth thinks of marriage as soon as she's in love with a man. Every woman, I don't care who she is.

Oh, if you were only married! It would be all the difference in the world. I think a child would do everything for you, Mona. Goodness knows, I just can't speak *decently* to that Garry, after the way he's treated you – well, you know perfectly well, *none* of your friends can – but I can frankly and honestly say, if he married you, I'd absolutely let bygones be bygones, and I'd be just as happy as happy, for you. If he's what you want. And I will say, what with your lovely looks and what with good-looking as he is, you ought to have simply *gorgeous* children. Mona, baby, you really have got a rotten cold, haven't you? Don't you want me to get you another handkerchief? Really?

I'm simply sick that I didn't bring you any flowers. But I thought the place would be full of them. Well, I'll stop on the way home and send you some. It looks too dreary here, without a flower in the room. Didn't Garry send you any? Oh, he didn't know you were sick. Well, doesn't he send you flowers anyway? Listen, hasn't he called up, all this time, and found out whether you were sick or not? Not in ten days? Well, then, haven't you called him and told him? Ah, now, Mona, there *is* such a thing as being too much of a heroine. Let him worry a little, dear. It would be a very good thing for him. Maybe that's the trouble – you've always taken all the worry for both of you. Hasn't sent any flowers! Hasn't even telephoned! Well, I'd just like to talk to that young man for a few minutes. After all, this is all *his* responsibility.

He's away? He's *what?* Oh, he went to Chicago two weeks ago. Well, it seems to me I'd always heard that there were telephone wires running between here and Chicago, but of course – And you'd think since he's been back, the least he could do would be to do something. He's not back yet? He's not *back* yet? Mona, what are you trying to tell me? Why, just night before last – Said he'd let you know the minute he got home? Of all the rotten, low things I ever heard in my life, this is really the – Mona, dear, please lie down. Please. Why, I didn't mean anything. I don't know what I was going to say, honestly I don't, it couldn't have been anything. For goodness' sake, let's talk about something else.

Let's see. Oh, you really ought to see Julia Post's living-room, the way she's done it now. She has brown walls – not beige, you know, or tan or anything, but brown – and these cream-colored taffeta curtains and – Mona, I tell you I absolutely don't know what I was going to say, before. It's gone completely out of my head. So you see how unimportant it must have been. Dear, please just lie quiet and try to relax. Please forget about that man for a few minutes, anyway. No man's worth getting that worked up about. Catch me doing it! You know you can't expect to get well quickly, if you get yourself so excited. You know that.

What doctor did you have, darling? Or don't you want to say? Your own? Your own Doctor Britton? You don't mean it! Well, I certainly never thought he'd do a thing like – Yes, dear, of course he's a nerve specialist. Yes, dear. Yes, dear. Yes, dear, of course you have perfect confidence in him. I only wish you would in me, once in a while; after we went to school together and everything. You might know I absolutely sympathize with you. I don't see how you could possibly have done anything else. I know you've always talked about how you'd give anything to have a baby, but it would have been so terribly unfair to the child to bring it into the world without being married. You'd have had to go live abroad and never see anybody and – And even then, somebody would have been sure to have told it sometime. They always do. You did the only possible thing, *I* think. Mona, for heaven's sake! Don't scream like that. I'm not deaf, you know. All right, dear, all right, all right, all right. All right, of course I believe you. Naturally I take your word for anything. Anything you say. Only please do try to be quiet. Just lie back and rest, and have a nice talk.

Ah, now don't keep harping on that. I've told you a hundred times, if I've told you once, I wasn't going to say anything at all. I tell you I don't remember *what* I was going to say. 'Night before last'? When did I mention 'night before last'? I never said any such – Well. Maybe it's better this way, Mona. The more I think of it, the more I think it's much better for you to hear it from me. Because somebody's bound to tell you. These things always come out. And I know you'd rather hear it from your oldest friend, wouldn't you? And the good Lord knows, anything I could do to make you see what that man really is! Only do relax, darling. Just for me. Dear, Garry isn't in Chicago. Fred and I saw him night before last at the Comet Club, dancing. And Alice saw him Tuesday night at El Rhumba. And I don't know how many people have said they've seen him around at the theater and night clubs and things. Why, he couldn't have stayed in Chicago more than a day or so – if he went at all.

Well, he was with *her* when we saw him, honey. Apparently he's with her all the time; nobody ever sees him with anyone else. You really must make up your mind to it, dear; it's the only thing to do. I hear all over that he's just simply *pleading* with her to marry him, but I don't know how true that is. I'm sure I can't see why he'd want to, but then you never can tell what a man like that will do. It would be just good enough *for* him if he got her, that's what *I* say. Then he'd see. She'd never stand for any of his nonsense. She'd make him toe the mark. She's a smart woman.

But, oh, so *ordinary*. I thought, when we saw them the other night, 'Well, she just looks cheap, that's all she looks.' That must be what he likes, I suppose. I must admit he looked very well. I never saw him look better. Of course you know what I think of him, but I always had to say he's one of the handsomest men I ever saw in my life. I can understand how any woman would be attracted to him – at first. Until they found out what he's really like. Oh, if you could have seen him with that awful, common creature, never once taking his eyes off her, and hanging on every word she said, as if it was pearls! It made me just—

Mona, angel, are you *crying?* Now, darling, that's just plain silly. That man's not worth another thought. You've thought about him entirely too much, that's the trouble.

Three years! Three of the best years of your life you've given him, and all the time he's been deceiving you with that woman. Just think back over what you've been through – all the times and times and times he promised you he'd give her up; and you, you poor little idiot, you'd believe him, and then he'd go right back to her again. And *everybody* knew about it. Think of that, and then try telling me that man's worth crying over! Really, Mona! I'd have more pride.

You know, I'm just glad this thing happened. I'm just glad you found out. This is a little too much, this time. In Chicago, indeed! Let you know the minute he came home! The kindest thing a person could possibly have done was to tell you, and bring you to your senses at last. I'm not sorry I did it, for a second. When I think of him out having the time of his life and you lying here deathly sick all on account of him, I could just – Yes, it is on account of him. Even if you didn't have an – well, even if I was mistaken about what I naturally thought was the matter with you when you made such a secret of your illness, he's driven you into a nervous breakdown, and that's plenty bad enough. All for that man! The skunk! You just put him right out of your head.

Why, of course you can, Mona. All you need to do is to pull yourself together, child. Simply say to yourself, 'Well, I've wasted three years of my life, and that's that.' Never worry about *him* any more. The Lord knows, darling, he's not worrying about you.

It's just because you're weak and sick that you're worked up like this, dear. I know. But you're going to be all right. You can make something of your life. You've got to, Mona, you know. Because after all – well, of course, you never looked sweeter, I don't mean that; but you're – well, you're not getting any younger. And here you've been throwing away your time, never seeing your friends, never going out, never meeting anybody new, just sitting here waiting for Garry to telephone, or Garry to come in – if he didn't have anything better to do. For three years, you've never had a thought in your head but that man. Now you just forget him.

Ah, baby, it isn't good for you to cry like that. Please don't. He's not even worth talking about. Look at the woman he's in love with, and you'll see what kind he is. You were much too good for him. You were much too sweet to him. You gave in too easily. The minute he had you, he didn't want you any more. That's what he's like. Why, he no more loved you than—

Mona, don't! Mona, stop it! Please, Mona! You mustn't talk like that, you mustn't say such things. You've got to stop crying, you'll be terribly sick. Stop, oh, stop it, oh, please stop! Oh, what am I going to do with her? Mona, dear – Mona! Oh, where in heaven's name is that fool maid?

Edie. Oh, Edie! Edie, I think you'd better get Dr Britton on the telephone, and tell him to come down and give Miss Morrison something to quiet her. I'm afraid she's got herself a little bit upset.

Big Blonde

I

Hazel Morse was a large, fair woman of the type that incites some men when they use the word 'blonde' to click their tongues and wag their heads roguishly. She prided herself upon her small feet and suffered for her vanity, boxing them in snub-toed, high-heeled slippers of the shortest bearable size. The curious things about her were her hands, strange terminations to the flabby white arms splattered with pale tan spots – long, quivering hands with deep and convex nails. She should not have disfigured them with little jewels.

She was not a woman given to recollections. At her middle thirties, her old days were a blurred and flickering sequence, an imperfect film, dealing with the actions of strangers.

In her twenties, after the deferred death of a hazy widowed mother, she had been employed as a model in a wholesale dress establishment – it was still the day of the big woman, and she was then prettily colored and erect and high-breasted. Her job was not onerous, and she met numbers of men and spent numbers of evenings with them, laughing at their jokes and telling them she loved their neckties. Men liked her, and she took it for granted that the liking of many men was a desirable thing. Popularity seemed to her to be worth all the work that had to be put into its achievement. Men liked you because you were fun, and when they liked you they took you out, and there you were. So, and successfully, she was fun. She was a good sport. Men like a good sport.

No other form of diversion, simpler or more complicated, drew her attention. She never pondered if she might not be better occupied doing something else. Her ideas, or, better, her acceptances, ran right along with those of the other substantially built blondes in whom she found her friends.

When she had been working in the dress establishment some years she met Herbie Morse. He was thin, quick, attractive, with shifting lines about his shiny, brown eyes and a habit of fiercely biting at the skin around his finger nails. He drank largely; she found that entertaining. Her habitual greeting to him was an allusion to his state of the previous night.

'Oh, what a peach you had,' she used to say, through her easy laugh. 'I thought I'd die, the way you kept asking the waiter to dance with you.'

She liked him immediately upon their meeting. She was enormously amused at his fast, slurred sentences, his interpolations of apt phrases from vaudeville acts and

119

comic strips; she thrilled at the feel of his lean arm tucked firm beneath the sleeve of her coat; she wanted to touch the wet, flat surface of his hair. He was as promptly drawn to her. They were married six weeks after they had met.

She was delighted at the idea of being a bride; coquetted with it, played upon it. Other offers of marriage she had had, and not a few of them, but it happened that they were all from stout, serious men who had visited the dress establishment as buyers; men from Des Moines and Houston and Chicago and, in her phrase, even funnier places. There was always something immensely comic to her in the thought of living elsewhere than New York. She could not regard as serious proposals that she share a western residence.

She wanted to be married. She was nearing thirty now, and she did not take the years well. She spread and softened, and her darkening hair turned her to inexpert dabblings with peroxide. There were times when she had little flashes of fear about her job. And she had had a couple of thousand evenings of being a good sport among her male acquaintances. She had come to be more conscientious than spontaneous about it.

Herbie earned enough, and they took a little apartment far uptown. There was a Mission-furnished dining-room with a hanging central light globed in liver-colored glass; in the living-room were an 'over-stuffed suite,' a Boston fern, and a reproduction of the Henner 'Magdalene' with the red hair and the blue draperies; the bedroom was in gray enamel and old rose, with Herbie's photograph on Hazel's dressing-table and Hazel's likeness on Herbie's chest of drawers.

She cooked – and she was a good cook – and marketed and chatted with the delivery boys and the colored laundress. She loved the flat, she loved her life, she loved Herbie. In the first months of their marriage, she gave him all the passion she was ever to know.

She had not realized how tired she was. It was a delight, a new game, a holiday, to give up being a good sport. If her head ached or her arches throbbed, she complained piteously, babyishly. If her mood was quiet, she did not talk. If tears came to her eyes, she let them fall.

She fell readily into the habit of tears during the first year of her marriage. Even in her good sport days, she had been known to weep lavishly and disinterestedly on occasion. Her behavior at the theater was a standing joke. She could weep at anything in a play – tiny garments, love both unrequited and mutual, seduction, purity, faithful servitors, wedlock, the triangle.

'There goes Haze,' her friends would say, watching her. 'She's off again.'

Wedded and relaxed, she poured her tears freely. To her who had laughed so much, crying was delicious. All sorrows became her sorrows; she was Tenderness. She would cry long and softly over newspaper accounts of kidnaped babies, deserted wives, unemployed men, strayed cats, heroic dogs. Even when the paper was no longer before her, her mind revolved upon these things and the drops slipped rhythmically over her plump cheeks.

'Honestly,' she would say to Herbie, 'all the sadness there is in the world when you stop to think about it!'

'Yeah,' Herbie would say.

She missed nobody. The old crowd, the people who had brought her and Herbie together, dropped from their lives, lingeringly at first. When she thought of this at all, it was only to consider it fitting. This was marriage. This was peace.

But the thing was that Herbie was not amused.

For a time, he had enjoyed being alone with her. He found the voluntary isolation novel and sweet. Then it palled with a ferocious suddenness. It was as if one night, sitting with her in the steam-heated living-room, he would ask no more; and the next night he was through and done with the whole thing.

He became annoyed by her misty melancholies. At first, when he came home to find her softly tired and moody, he kissed her neck and patted her shoulder and begged her to tell her Herbie what was wrong. She loved that. But time slid by, and he found that there was never anything really, personally, the matter.

'Ah, for God's sake,' he would say. 'Crabbing again. All right, sit here and crab your head off. I'm going out.'

And he would slam out of the flat and come back late and drunk.

She was completely bewildered by what happened to

their marriage. First they were lovers; and then, it seemed without transition, they were enemies. She never understood it.

There were longer and longer intervals between his leaving his office and his arrival at the apartment. She went through agonies of picturing him run over and bleeding, dead and covered with a sheet. Then she lost her fears for his safety and grew sullen and wounded. When a person wanted to be with a person, he came as soon as possible. She desperately wanted him to want to be with her; her own hours only marked the time till he would come. It was often nearly nine o'clock before he came home to dinner. Always he had had many drinks, and their effect would die in him, leaving him loud and querulous and bristling for affronts.

He was too nervous, he said, to sit and do nothing for an evening. He boasted, probably not in all truth, that he had never read a book in his life.

'What am I expected to do – sit around this dump on my tail all night?' he would ask, rhetorically. And again he would slam out.

She did not know what to do. She could not manage him. She could not meet him.

She fought him furiously. A terrific domesticity had come upon her, and she would bite and scratch to guard it. She wanted what she called 'a nice home.' She wanted a sober, tender husband, prompt at dinner, punctual at work. She wanted sweet, comforting evenings. The idea of intimacy with other men was terrible to her; the thought that Herbie might be seeking entertainment in other women set her frantic.

It seemed to her that almost everything she read – novels from the drug-store lending library, magazine stories, women's pages in the papers – dealt with wives who lost their husbands' love. She could bear those, at that, better than accounts of neat, companionable marriage and living happily ever after.

She was frightened. Several times when Herbie came home in the evening, he found her determinedly dressed – she had had to alter those of her clothes that were not new, to make them fasten – and rouged.

'Let's go wild tonight, what do you say?' she would hail him. 'A person's got lots of time to hang around and do nothing when they're dead.'

So they would go out, to chop houses and the less expensive cabarets. But it turned out badly. She could no longer find amusement in watching Herbie drink. She could not laugh at his whimsicalities, she was so tensely counting his indulgences. And she was unable to keep back her remonstrances – 'Ah, come on, Herb, you've had enough, haven't you? You'll feel something terrible in the morning.'

He would be immediately enraged. All right, crab; crab, crab, crab, crab, that was all she ever did. What a lousy sport *she* was! There would be scenes, and one or the other of them would rise and stalk out in fury.

She could not recall the definite day that she started drinking, herself. There was nothing separate about her days. Like drops upon a window-pane, they ran together and trickled away. She had been married six months; then a year; then three years.

She had never needed to drink, formerly. She could sit for most of a night at a table where the others were imbibing earnestly and never droop in looks or spirits, nor be bored by the doings of those about her. If she took a cocktail, it was so unusual as to cause twenty minutes or so of jocular comment. But now anguish was in her. Frequently, after a quarrel, Herbie would stay out for the night, and she could not learn from him where the time had been spent. Her heart felt tight and sore in her breast, and her mind turned like an electric fan.

She hated the taste of liquor. Gin, plain or in mixtures, made her promptly sick. After experiment, she found that Scotch whisky was best for her. She took it without water, because that was the quickest way to its effect.

Herbie pressed it on her. He was glad to see her drink. They both felt it might restore her high spirits, and their good times together might again be possible.

' 'Atta girl,' he would approve her. 'Let's see you get boiled, baby.'

But it brought them no nearer. When she drank with him, there would be a little while of gaiety and then, strangely without beginning, they would be in a wild quarrel. They would wake in the morning not sure what it had all been about, foggy as to what had been said and done, but each deeply injured and bitterly resentful. There would be days of vengeful silence.

There had been a time when they had made up their quarrels, usually in bed. There would be kisses and little names and assurances of fresh starts . . . 'Oh, it's going to be great now, Herb. We'll have swell times. I was a crab. I guess I must have been tired. But everything's going to be swell. You'll see.'

Now there were no gentle reconciliations. They resumed friendly relations only in the brief magnanimity caused by liquor, before more liquor drew them into new battles. The scenes became more violent. There were shouted invectives and pushes, and sometimes sharp slaps. Once she had a black eye. Herbie was horrified next day at sight of it. He did not go to work; he followed her about, suggesting remedies and heaping dark blame on himself. But after they had had a few drinks – 'to pull themselves together' – she made so many wistful references to her bruise that he shouted at her and rushed out and was gone for two days.

Each time he left the place in a rage, he threatened never to come back. She did not believe him, nor did she consider separation. Somewhere in her head or her heart was the lazy, nebulous hope that things would change and she and Herbie settle suddenly into soothing married life. Here were her home, her furniture, her husband, her station. She summoned no alternatives.

She could no longer bustle and potter. She had no more vicarious tears; the hot drops she shed were for herself. She walked ceaselessly about the rooms, her thoughts running mechanically round and round Herbie. In those days began the hatred of being alone that she was never to overcome. You could be by yourself when things were all right, but when you were blue you got the howling horrors.

She commenced drinking alone, little, short drinks all through the day. It was only with Herbie that alcohol made her nervous and quick in offense. Alone, it blurred sharp things for her. She lived in a haze of it. Her life took on a dream-like quality. Nothing was astonishing.

A Mrs Martin moved into the flat across the hall. She was a great blonde woman of forty, a promise in looks of what Mrs Morse was to be. They made acquaintance, quickly became inseparable. Mrs Morse spent her days in the opposite apartment. They drank together, to brace themselves after the drinks of the nights before.

She never confided her troubles about Herbie to Mrs Martin. The subject was too bewildering to her to find comfort in talk. She let it be assumed that her husband's business kept him much away. It was not regarded as important; husbands, as such, played but shadowy parts in Mrs Martin's circle.

Mrs Martin had no visible spouse; you were left to decide for yourself whether he was or was not dead. She had an admirer, Joe, who came to see her almost nightly. Often he brought several friends with him – 'The Boys,' they were called. The Boys were big, red, good-humored men, perhaps forty-five, perhaps fifty. Mrs Morse was glad of invitations to join the parties – Herbie was scarcely ever at home at night now. If he did come home, she did not visit Mrs Martin. An evening alone with Herbie meant inevitably a quarrel, yet she would stay with him. There was always her thin and wordless idea that, maybe, this night, things would begin to be all right.

The Boys brought plenty of liquor along with them whenever they came to Mrs Martin's. Drinking with them, Mrs Morse became lively and good-natured and audacious. She was quickly popular. When she had drunk enough to cloud her most recent battle with Herbie, she was excited by their approbation. Crab, was she? Rotten sport, was she? Well, there were some that thought different.

Ed was one of The Boys. He lived in Utica – had 'his own business' there, was the awed report – but he came to New York almost every week. He was married. He showed Mrs Morse the then current photographs of Junior and Sister, and she praised them abundantly and sincerely. Soon it was accepted by the others that Ed was her particular friend.

He staked her when they all played poker; sat next her and occasionally rubbed his knee against hers during the game. She was rather lucky. Frequently she went home with a twenty-dollar bill or a ten-dollar bill or a handful of crumpled dollars. She was glad of them. Herbie was getting, in her words, something awful about money. To ask him for it brought an instant row.

'What the hell do you do with it?' he would say. 'Shoot it all on Scotch?'

'I try to run this house half-way decent,' she would retort. 'Never thought of that, did you? Oh, no, his lordship couldn't be bothered with that.'

Again, she could not find a definite day, to fix the beginning of Ed's proprietorship. It became his custom to kiss her on the mouth when he came in, as well as for farewell, and he gave her little quick kisses of approval all through the evening. She liked this rather more than she disliked it. She never thought of his kisses when she was not with him.

He would run his hand lingeringly over her back and shoulders.

'Some dizzy blonde, eh?' he would say. 'Some doll.'

One afternoon she came home from Mrs Martin's to find Herbie in the bedroom. He had been away for several nights, evidently on a prolonged drinking bout. His face was gray, his hands jerked as if they were on wires. On the bed were two old suitcases, packed high. Only her photograph remained on his bureau, and the wide doors of his closet disclosed nothing but coat-hangers.

'I'm blowing,' he said. 'I'm through with the whole works. I got a job in Detroit.'

She sat down on the edge of the bed. She had drunk much the night before, and the four Scotches she had had with Mrs Martin had only increased her fogginess.

'Good job?' she said.

'Oh, yeah,' he said. 'Looks all right.'

He closed a suitcase with difficulty, swearing at it in whispers.

'There's some dough in the bank,' he said. 'The bank book's in your top drawer. You can have the furniture and stuff.'

He looked at her, and his forehead twitched.

'God damn it, I'm through, I'm telling you,' he cried. 'I'm through.'

'All right, all right,' she said. 'I heard you, didn't I?'

She saw him as if he were at one end of a cannon and she at the other. Her head was beginning to ache bumpingly, and her voice had a dreary, tiresome tone. She could not have raised it.

'Like a drink before you go?' she asked.

Again he looked at her, and a corner of his mouth jerked up.

'Cockeyed again for a change, aren't you?' he said. 'That's nice. Sure, get a couple of shots, will you?'

She went to the pantry, mixed him a stiff highball, poured herself a couple of inches of whisky and drank it. Then she gave herself another portion and brought the glasses into the bedroom. He had strapped both suitcases and had put on his hat and overcoat.

He took his highball.

'Well,' he said, and he gave a sudden, uncertain laugh. 'Here's mud in your eye.'

'Mud in your eye,' she said.

They drank. He put down his glass and took up the heavy suitcases.

'Got to get a train around six,' he said.

She followed him down the hall. There was a song, a song that Mrs Martin played doggedly on the phonograph, running loudly through her mind. She had never liked the thing.

> 'Night and daytime,
> Always playtime.
> Ain't we got fun?'

At the door he put down the bags and faced her.

'Well,' he said. 'Well, take care of yourself. You'll be all right, will you?'

'Oh, sure,' she said.

He opened the door, then came back to her, holding out his hand.

''By, Haze,' he said. 'Good luck to you.'

She took his hand and shook it.

'Pardon my wet glove,' she said.

When the door had closed behind him, she went back to the pantry.

She was flushed and lively when she went in to Mrs Martin's that evening. The Boys were there, Ed among them. He was glad to be in town, frisky and loud and full of jokes. But she spoke quietly to him for a minute.

'Herbie blew today,' she said. 'Going to live out west.'

'That so?' he said. He looked at her and played with the fountain pen clipped to his waistcoat pocket.

'Think he's gone for good, do you?' he asked.

'Yeah,' she said. 'I know he is. I know. Yeah.'

'You going to live on across the hall just the same?' he said. 'Know what you're going to do?'

'Gee, I don't know,' she said. 'I don't give much of a damn.'

'Oh, come on, that's no way to talk,' he told her. 'What you need – you need a little snifter. How about it?'

'Yeah,' she said. 'Just straight.'

She won forty-three dollars at poker. When the game broke up, Ed took her back to her apartment.

'Got a little kiss for me?' he asked.

He wrapped her in his big arms and kissed her violently. She was entirely passive. He held her away and looked at her.

'Little tight, honey?' he asked, anxiously. 'Not going to be sick, are you?'

'Me?' she said. 'I'm swell.'

II

When Ed left in the morning, he took her photograph with him. He said he wanted her picture to look at, up in Utica. 'You can have that one on the bureau,' she said.

She put Herbie's picture in a drawer, out of her sight.

When she could look at it, she meant to tear it up. She was fairly successful in keeping her mind from racing around him. Whisky slowed it for her. She was almost peaceful, in her mist.

She accepted her relationship with Ed without question or enthusiasm. When he was away, she seldom thought definitely of him. He was good to her; he gave her frequent presents and a regular allowance. She was even able to save. She did not plan ahead of any day, but her wants were few, and you might as well put money in the bank as have it lying around.

When the lease of her apartment neared its end, it was Ed who suggested moving. His friendship with Mrs Martin and Joe had become strained over a dispute at poker; a feud was impending.

'Let's get the hell out of here,' Ed said. 'What I want you to have is a place near the Grand Central. Make it easier for me.'

So she took a little flat in the Forties. A colored maid came in every day to clean and to make coffee for her – she was 'through with that housekeeping stuff,' she said, and Ed, twenty years married to a passionately domestic woman, admired this romantic uselessness and felt doubly a man of the world in abetting it.

The coffee was all she had until she went out to dinner, but alcohol kept her fat. Prohibition she regarded only as a basis for jokes. You could always get all you wanted. She was never noticeably drunk and seldom nearly sober.

It required a larger daily allowance to keep her misty-minded. Too little, and she was achingly melancholy.

Ed brought her to Jimmy's. He was proud, with the pride of the transient who would be mistaken for a native, in his knowledge of small, recent restaurants occupying the lower floors of shabby brownstone houses; places where, upon mentioning the name of an habitué friend, might be obtained strange whisky and fresh gin in many of their ramifications. Jimmy's place was the favorite of his acquaintances.

There, through Ed, Mrs Morse met many men and women, formed quick friendships. The men often took her out when Ed was in Utica. He was proud of her popularity.

She fell into the habit of going to Jimmy's alone when she had no engagement. She was certain to meet some people she knew, and join them. It was a club for her friends, both men and women.

The women at Jimmy's looked remarkably alike, and this was curious, for, through feuds, removals, and opportunities of more profitable contacts, the personnel of the group changed constantly. Yet always the newcomers resembled those whom they replaced. They were all big women and stout, broad of shoulder and abundantly breasted, with faces thickly clothed in soft, high-colored flesh. They laughed loud and often, showing opaque and lusterless teeth like squares of crockery. There was about them the health of the big, yet a slight, unwholesome suggestion of stubborn preservation. They might have been thirty-six or forty-five or anywhere between.

They composed their titles of their own first names with their husbands' surnames – Mrs Florence Miller, Mrs Vera Riley, Mrs Lilian Block. This gave at the same time the solidity of marriage and the glamour of freedom. Yet only one or two were actually divorced. Most of them never referred to their dimmed spouses; some, a shorter time separated, described them in terms of great biological interest. Several were mothers, each of an only child – a boy at school somewhere, or a girl being cared for by a grandmother. Often, well on towards morning, there would be displays of kodak portaits and of tears.

They were comfortable women, cordial and friendly and irrepressibly matronly. Theirs was the quality of ease. Become fatalistic, especially about money matters, they were unworried. Whenever their funds dropped alarmingly, a new donor appeared; this had always happened. The aim of each was to have one man, permanently, to pay all her bills, in return for which she would have immediately given up other admirers and probably would have become exceedingly fond of him; for the affections of all of them were, by now, unexacting, tranquil, and easily arranged. This end, however, grew increasingly difficult yearly. Mrs Morse was regarded as fortunate.

Ed had a good year, increased her allowance and gave her a sealskin coat. But she had to be careful of her moods with him. He insisted upon gaiety. He would not listen to admissions of aches or weariness.

'Hey, listen,' he would say, 'I got worries of my own, and plenty. Nobody wants to hear other people's troubles, sweetie. What you got to do, you got to be a sport and forget it. See? Well, slip us a little smile, then. That's my girl.'

She never had enough interest to quarrel with him as she had with Herbie, but she wanted the privilege of occasional admitted sadness. It was strange. The other women she saw did not have to fight their moods. There was Mrs Florence Miller who got regular crying jags, and the men sought only to cheer and comfort her. The others spent whole evenings in grieved recitals of worries and ills; their escorts paid them deep sympathy. But she was instantly undesirable when she was low in spirits. Once, at Jimmy's, when she could not make herself lively, Ed had walked out and left her.

'Why the hell don't you stay home and not go spoiling everybody's evening?' he had roared.

Even her slightest acquaintances seemed irritated if she were not conspicuously light-hearted.

'What's the matter with you, anyway?' they would say. 'Be your age, why don't you? Have a little drink and snap out of it.'

When her relationship with Ed had continued nearly three years, he moved to Florida to live. He hated leaving her; he gave her a large check and some shares of a sound stock, and his pale eyes were wet when he said good-by. She did not miss him. He came to New York infrequently, perhaps two or three times a year, and hurried directly from the train to see her. She was always pleased to have him come and never sorry to see him go.

Charley, an acquaintance of Ed's that she had met at Jimmy's, had long admired her. He had always made opportunities of touching her and learning close to talk to her. He asked repeatedly of all their friends if they had ever heard such a fine laugh as she had. After Ed left, Charley became the main figure in her life. She classified him and spoke of him as 'not so bad.' There was nearly a year of Charley; then she divided her time between him and Sydney, another frequenter of Jimmy's; then Charley slipped away altogether.

Sydney was a little, brightly dressed, clever Jew. She was perhaps nearest contentment with him. He amused her always; her laughter was not forced.

He admired her completely. Her softness and size delighted him. And he thought she was great, he often told her, because she kept gay and lively when she was drunk.

'Once I had a gal,' he said, 'used to try and throw herself out of the window every time she got a can on. Jee-*zuss*,' he added, feelingly.

Then Sydney married a rich and watchful bride, and then there was Billy. No – after Sydney came Ferd, then Billy. In her haze, she never recalled how men entered her life and left it. There were no surprises. She had no thrill at their advent, nor woe at their departure. She seemed to be always able to attract men. There was never another as rich as Ed, but they were all generous to her, in their means.

Once she had news of Herbie. She met Mrs Martin dining at Jimmy's, and the old friendship was vigorously renewed. The still admiring Joe, while on a business trip, had seen Herbie. He had settled in Chicago, he looked fine, he was living with some woman – seemed to be crazy about her. Mrs Morse had been drinking vastly that day. She took the news with mild interest, as one hearing of the sex peccadilloes of somebody whose name is, after a moment's groping, familiar.

'Must be damn near seven years since I saw him,' she commented. 'Gee. Seven years.'

More and more, her days lost their individuality. She never knew dates, nor was sure of the day of the week.

'My God, was that a year ago!' she would exclaim, when an event was recalled in conversation.

She was tired so much of the time. Tired and blue. Almost everything could give her the blues. Those old horses she saw on Sixth Avenue – struggling and slipping along the car-tracks, or standing at the curb, their heads dropped level with their worn knees. The tightly stored tears would squeeze from her eyes as she teetered past on her aching feet in the stubby, champagne-colored slippers.

The thought of death came and stayed with her and lent her a sort of drowsy cheer. It would be nice, nice and restful, to be dead.

There was no settled, shocked moment when she first thought of killing herself; it seemed to her as if the idea had always been with her. She pounced upon all the accounts of suicides in the newspapers. There was an epidemic of self-killings – or maybe it was just that she searched for the stories of them so eagerly that she found many. To read of them roused reassurance in her; she felt a cozy solidarity with the big company of the voluntary dead.

She slept, aided by whisky, till deep into the afternoons, then lay abed, a bottle and glass at her hand, until it was time to dress to go out for dinner. She was beginning to feel towards alcohol a little puzzled distrust, as toward an old friend who has refused a simple favor. Whisky could still soothe her for most of the time, but there were sudden, inexplicable moments when the cloud fell treacherously away from her, and she was sawed by the sorrow and bewilderment and nuisance of all living. She played voluptuously with the thought of cool, sleepy retreat. She had never been troubled by religious belief and no vision of an after-life intimidated her. She dreamed by day of never again putting on tight shoes, of never having to laugh and listen and admire, of never more being a good sport. Never.

But how would you do it? It made her sick to think of

jumping from heights. She could not stand a gun. At the theater, if one of the actors drew a revolver, she crammed her fingers into her ears and could not even look at the stage until after the shot had been fired. There was no gas in her flat. She looked long at the bright blue veins in her slim wrists – a cut with a razor blade, and there you'd be. But it would hurt, hurt like hell, and there would be blood to see. Poison – something tasteless and quick and painless – was the thing. But they wouldn't sell it to you in drugstores, because of the law.

She had few other thoughts.

There was a new man now – Art. He was short and fat and exacting and hard on her patience when he was drunk. But there had been only occasionals for some time before him, and she was glad of a little stability. Too, Art must be away for weeks at a stretch, selling silks, and that was restful. She was convincingly gay with him, though the effort shook her.

'The best sport in the world,' he would murmur, deep in her neck. 'The best sport in the world.'

One night, when he had taken her to Jimmy's, she went into the dressing-room with Mrs Florence Miller. There, while designing curly mouths on their faces with lip-rouge, they compared experiences of insomnia.

'Honestly,' Mrs Morse said, 'I wouldn't close an eye if I didn't go to bed full of Scotch. I lie there and toss and turn and toss and turn. Blue! Does a person get blue lying awake that way!'

'Say, listen Hazel,' Mrs Miller said, impressively, 'I'm telling you I'd be awake for a year if I didn't take veronal. That stuff makes you sleep like a fool.'

'Isn't it poison, or something?' Mrs Morse asked.

'Oh, you take too much and you're out for count,' said Mrs Miller. 'I just take five grains – they come in tablets. I'd be scared to fool around with it. But five grains, and you cork off pretty.'

'Can you get it anywhere?' Mrs Morse felt superbly Machiavellian.

'Get all you want in Jersey,' said Mrs Miller. 'They won't give it to you here without you have a doctor's prescription. Finished? We'd better go back and see what the boys are doing.'

That night, Art left Mrs Morse at the door of her apartment; his mother was in town. Mrs Morse was still sober, and it happened that there was no whisky left in her cupboard. She lay in bed, looking up at the black ceiling.

She rose early, for her, and went to New Jersey. She had never taken the tube, and did not understand it. So she went to the Pennsylvania Station and bought a railroad ticket to Newark. She thought of nothing in particular on the trip out. She looked at the uninspired hats of the women about her and gazed through the smeared window at the flat, gritty scene.

In Newark, in the first drug-store she came to, she asked for a tin of talcum powder, a nailbrush, and a box of veronal tablets. The powder and the brush were to make the hypnotic seem also a casual need. The clerk was entirely unconcerned. 'We only keep them in bottles,' he said, and wrapped up for her a little glass vial containing ten white tablets, stacked one on another.

She went to another drug-store and bought a face-cloth, an orange-wood stick, and a bottle of veronal tablets. The clerk was also uninterested.

'Well, I guess I got enough to kill an ox,' she thought, and went back to the station.

At home, she put the little vials in the drawer of her dressing-table and stood looking at them with a dreamy tenderness.

'There they are, God bless them,' she said, and she kissed her fingertip and touched each bottle.

The colored maid was busy in the living-room.

'Hey, Nettie,' Mrs Morse called. 'Be an angel, will you? Run around to Jimmy's and get me a quart of Scotch.'

She hummed while she awaited the girl's return.

During the next few days, whisky ministered to her as tenderly as it had done when she first turned to its aid. Alone, she was soothed and vague, at Jimmy's she was the gayest of the groups. Art was delighted with her.

Then, one night, she had an appointment to meet Art at Jimmy's for an early dinner. He was to leave afterward on a business excursion, to be away for a week. Mrs Morse had been drinking all the afternoon; while she dressed to go out, she felt herself rising pleasurably from drowsiness to high spirits. But as she came out into the street the effects of the whisky deserted her completely, and she was filled with a slow, grinding wretchedness so horrible that she stood swaying on the pavement, unable for a moment to move forward. It was a gray night with spurts of mean, thin snow, and the streets shone with dark ice. As she slowly crossed Sixth Avenue, consciously dragging one foot past the other, a big, scarred horse pulling a rickety express-wagon crashed to his knees before her. The driver swore and screamed and lashed the beast insanely, bringing the whip back over his shoulder for every blow, while the horse struggled to get a footing on the slippery asphalt. A group gathered and watched with interest.

Art was waiting, when Mrs Morse reached Jimmy's.

'What's the matter with you, for God's sake?' was his greeting to her.

'I saw a horse,' she said. 'Gee, I – a person feels sorry for horses. I – it isn't just horses. Everything's kind of terrible, isn't it? I can't help getting sunk.'

'Ah, sunk, me eye,' he said. 'What's the idea of all the bellyaching? What have you got to be sunk about?'

'I can't help it,' she said.

'Ah, help it, me eye,' he said. 'Pull yourself together, will you? Come on and sit down, and take that face off you.'

She drank industriously and she tried hard, but she could not overcome her melancholy. Others joined them and commented on her gloom, and she could do no more for them than smile weakly. She made little dabs at her eyes with her handkerchief, trying to time her movements so they would be unnoticed, but several times Art caught her and scowled and shifted impatiently in his chair.

When it was time for him to go to his train, she said she would leave, too, and go home.

'And not a bad idea, either,' he said. 'See if you can't sleep yourself out of it. I'll see you Thursday. For God's sake, try and cheer up by then, will you?'

'Yeah,' she said. 'I will.'

In her bedroom, she undressed with a tense speed wholly unlike her usual slow uncertainty. She put on her nightgown, took off her hair-net and passed the comb quickly through her dry, vari-colored hair. Then she took the two little vials from the drawer and carried them into the bathroom. The splintering misery had gone from her, and she felt the quick excitement of one who is about to receive an anticipated gift.

She uncorked the vials, filled a glass with water and stood before the mirror, a tablet between her fingers. Suddenly she bowed graciously to her reflection, and raised the glass to it.

'Well, here's mud in your eye,' she said.

The tablets were unpleasant to take, dry and powdery and sticking obstinately half-way down her throat. It took her a long time to swallow all twenty of them. She stood watching her reflection with deep, impersonal interest, studying the movements of the gulping throat. Once more she spoke aloud.

'For God's sake, try and cheer up by Thursday, will you?' she said. 'Well, you know what he can do. He and the whole lot of them.'

She had no idea how quickly to expect effect from the veronal. When she had taken the last tablet, she stood uncertainly, wondering, still with a courteous, vicarious interest, if death would strike her down then and there. She felt in no way strange, save for a slight stirring of sickness from the effort of swallowing the tablets, nor did her reflected face look at all different. It would not be immediate, then; it might even take an hour or so.

She stretched her arms high and gave a vast yawn.

'Guess I'll go to bed,' she said. 'Gee, I'm nearly dead.'

That struck her as comic, and she turned out the bathroom light and went in and laid herself down in her bed, chuckling softly all the time.

'Gee, I'm nearly dead,' she quoted. 'That's a hot one!'

III

Nettie, the colored maid, came in late the next afternoon to clean the apartment, and found Mrs Morse in her bed. But then, that was not unusual. Usually, though, the sounds of cleaning waked her, and she did not like to wake up. Nettie, an agreeable girl, had learned to move softly about her work.

But when she had done the living-room and stolen in

to tidy the little square bedroom, she could not avoid a tiny clatter as she arranged the objects on the dressing-table. Instinctively, she glanced over her shoulder at the sleeper, and without warning a sickly uneasiness crept over her. She came to the bed and stared down at the woman lying there.

Mrs Morse lay on her back, one flabby, white arm flung up, the wrist against her forehead. Her stiff hair hung untenderly along her face. The bed covers were pushed down, exposing a deep square of soft neck and a pink nightgown, its fabric worn uneven by many launderings; her great breasts, freed from their tight confiner, sagged beneath her armpits. Now and then she made knotted, snoring sounds, and from the corner of her opened mouth to the blurred turn of her jaw ran a lane of crusted spittle.

'Mis' Morse,' Nettie called. 'Oh, Mis' Morse! It's terrible late.'

Mrs Morse made no move.

'Mis' Morse,' said Nettie. 'Look, Mis' Morse. How'm I goin' get this bed made?'

Panic sprang upon the girl. She shook the woman's hot shoulder.

'Ah, wake up, will yuh?' she whined. 'Ah, please wake up.'

Suddenly the girl turned and ran out in the hall to the elevator door, keeping her thumb firm on the black, shiny button until the elderly car and its Negro attendant stood

before her. She poured a jumble of words over the boy,
and led him back to the apartment. He tiptoed creakingly
in to the bedside; first gingerly, then so lustily that he left
marks in the soft flesh, he prodded the unconscious
woman.

'Hey, there!' he cried, and listened intently, as for an
echo.

'Jeez. Out like a light,' he commented.

At his interest in the spectacle, Nettie's panic left her.
Importance was big in both of them. They talked in quick,
unfinished whispers, and it was the boy's suggestion that
he fetch the young doctor who lived on the ground floor.
Nettie hurried along with him. They looked forward to
the limelit moment of breaking their news of something
untoward, something pleasurably unpleasant. Mrs Morse
had become the medium of drama. With no ill wish to
her, they hoped that her state was serious, that she would
not let them down by being awake and normal on their
return. A little fear of this determined them to make the
most, to the doctor, of her present condition. 'Matter of
life and death,' returned to Nettie from her thin store of
reading. She considered startling the doctor with the
phrase.

The doctor was in and none too pleased at interrup-
tion. He wore a yellow and blue striped dressing-gown,
and he was lying on his sofa, laughing with a dark girl,
her face scaly with inexpensive powder, who perched on
the arm. Half-emptied highball glasses stood beside them,

and her coat and hat were neatly hung up with the comfortable implication of a long stay.

Always something, the doctor grumbled. Couldn't let anybody alone after a hard day. But he put some bottles and instruments into a case, changed his dressing-gown for his coat and started out with the Negroes.

'Snap it up there, big boy,' the girl called after him. 'Don't be all night.'

The doctor strode loudly into Mrs Morse's flat and on to the bedroom, Nettie and the boy right behind him. Mrs Morse had not moved; her sleep was as deep, but soundless, now. The doctor looked sharply at her, then plunged his thumbs into the lidded pits above her eyeballs and threw his weight upon them. A high, sickened cry broke from Nettie.

'Look like he tryin' to push her right on th'ough the bed,' said the boy. He chuckled.

Mrs Morse gave no sign under the pressure. Abruptly the doctor abandoned it, and with one quick movement swept the covers down to the foot of the bed. With another he flung her nightgown back and lifted the thick, white legs, cross-hatched with blocks of tiny, iris-colored veins. He pinched them repeatedly, with long, cruel nips, back of the knees. She did not awaken.

'What's she been drinking?' he asked Nettie, over his shoulder.

With the certain celerity of one who knows just where

to lay hands on a thing, Nettie went into the bathroom, bound for the cupboard where Mrs Morse kept her whisky. But she stopped at the sight of the two vials, with their red and white labels, lying before the mirror. She brought them to the doctor.

'Oh, for the Lord Almighty's sweet sake!' he said. He dropped Mrs Morse's legs, and pushed them impatiently across the bed. 'What did she want to go taking that tripe for? Rotten yellow trick, that's what a thing like that is. Now we'll have to pump her out, and all that stuff. Nuisance, a thing like that is; that's what it amounts to. Here, George, take me down in the elevator. You wait here, maid. She won't do anything.'

'She won't die on me, will she?' cried Nettie.

'No,' said the doctor. 'God, no. You couldn't kill her with an ax.'

IV

After two days, Mrs Morse came back to consciousness, dazed at first, then with a comprehension that brought with it the slow, saturating wretchedness.

'Oh, Lord, oh, Lord,' she moaned, and tears for herself and for life striped her cheeks.

Nettie came in at the sound. For two days she had done the ugly, incessant tasks in the nursing of the unconscious, for two nights she had caught broken bits of sleep on the living-room couch. She looked coldly at the big, blown woman in the bed.

'What you been tryin' to do, Mis' Morse?' she said. 'What kine o' work is that, takin' all that stuff?'

'Oh, Lord,' moaned Mrs Morse, again, and she tried to cover her eyes with her arms. But the joints felt stiff and brittle, and she cried out at their ache.

'Tha's no way to ack, takin' them pills,' said Nettie. 'You can thank you' stars you heah at all. How you feel now?'

'Oh, I feel great,' said Mrs Morse. 'Swell, I feel.'

Her hot, painful tears fell as if they would never stop.

'Tha's no way to take on, cryin' like that,' Nettie said. 'After what you done. The doctor, he says he could have you arrested, doin' a thing like that. He was fit to be tied, here.'

'Why couldn't he let me alone?' wailed Mrs Morse. 'Why the hell couldn't he have?'

'Tha's terr'ble, Mis' Morse, swearin' an' talkin' like that,' said Nettie, 'after what people done for you. Here I ain' had no sleep at all for two nights, an' had to give up goin' out to my other ladies!'

'Oh, I'm sorry, Nettie,' she said. 'You're a peach. I'm sorry I've given you so much trouble. I couldn't help it. I just got sunk. Didn't you ever feel like doing it? When everything looks just lousy to you?'

'I wouldn' think o' no such thing,' declared Nettie.

'You got to cheer up. Tha's what you got to do. Every-body's got their troubles.'

'Yeah,' said Mrs Morse. 'I know.'

'Come a pretty picture card for you,' Nettie said. 'Maybe that will cheer you up.'

She handed Mrs Morse a post-card. Mrs Morse had to cover one eye with her hand, in order to read the message; her eyes were not yet focusing correctly.

It was from Art. On the back of a view of the Detroit Athletic Club he had written: 'Greeting and salutations. Hope you have lost that gloom. Cheer up and don't take any rubber nickles. See you on Thursday.'

She dropped the card to the floor. Misery crushed her as if she were between great smooth stones. There passed before her a slow, slow pageant of days spent lying in her flat, of evenings at Jimmy's being a good sport, making herself laugh and coo at Art and other Arts; she saw a long parade of weary horses and shivering beggars and all beaten, driven, stumbling things. Her feet throbbed as if she had crammed them into the stubby champagne-colored slippers. Her heart seemed to swell and harden.

'Nettie,' she cried, 'for heaven's sake pour me a drink, will you?'

The maid looked doubtful.

'Now you know, Mis' Morse,' she said, 'you been near daid. I don' know if the doctor he let you drink nothin' yet.'

'Oh, never mind him,' she said. 'You get me one, and bring in the bottle. Take one yourself.'

'Well,' said Nettie.

She poured them each a drink, deferentially leaving hers in the bathroom to be taken in solitude, and brought Mrs Morse's glass in to her.

Mrs Morse looked into the liquor and shuddered back from its odor. Maybe it would help. Maybe, when you had been knocked cold for a few days, your very first drink would give you a lift. Maybe whisky would be her friend again. She prayed without addressing a God, without knowing a God. Oh, please, please, let her be able to get drunk, please keep her always drunk.

She lifted the glass.

'Thanks, Nettie,' she said. 'Here's mud in your eye.'

The maid giggled. 'Tha's the way, Mis' Morse,' she said. 'You cheer up, now.'

'Yeah,' said Mrs Morse. 'Sure.'